"Don't you remember what it was like to be seventeen?"

Their gazes collided across space and time. At seventeen Bruce had been her whole world. He'd broken her heart then and he'd broken it again later. Both times because he'd chosen the Marine Corps over her.

"No," he denied, taking the stapler from her. The brush of his hand took Mitzi by surprise. Every scarred knuckle, every callus on his palm was as familiar to her as the memory of his touch.

"Me either," she lied. Heaven help her, she wasn't seventeen anymore and it was hard for *her* to resist.

But resist him she would.

Dear Reader,

Sometimes a story starts with a spark and other times it takes several sparks to set off that explosion, as was the case with Gunnery Sgt. Bruce Calhoun, USMC. June 20, 2003, marked the beginning of a year-long trial in which eighty-one Marines and five Navy hospital corpsman began training to integrate into Navy SEAL teams. Also, the wounded started coming home from war and amputees returning to duty were making headlines. In those cumulating events I discovered my hero.

I chose the city of Englewood in the shadow of Denver, Colorado, for its small-town feel. The VA hospital mentioned in this story is fictional—the real one is in Denver.

That detail isn't the only blurring of reality and fiction. The Englewood Navy Recruiting Station, where I enlisted and worked as a receptionist before shipping off to boot camp, no longer exists. Including a JROTC program as part of the high school curriculum was a stretch because Junior Reserve Officers Training Corps is offered in Denver schools. I made the compromise because JROTC was an important part of my formative years.

I wanted to give my Marine a nice, cushy desk job in a state with a small Marine contingent so making him a recruiter seemed like a good option. Cushy being tongue-in-cheek as the job of a recruiter is not an easy one.

As for his heroine, Navy recruiter, Chief Petty Officer Mitzi Zahn, I didn't have to look farther than a margin note in a previous manuscript by my editor, Victoria Curran. She wanted to know more about the high school sweetheart who ran from his hospital room. The idea intrigued and as I wrote, I discovered exactly what these two characters were running from—and toward.
I hope you enjoy their journey.

You can contact me via my website
www.rogennabrewer.com.

Rogenna Brewer

Mitzi's Marine
Rogenna Brewer

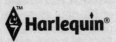

TORONTO NEW YORK LONDON
AMSTERDAM PARIS SYDNEY HAMBURG
STOCKHOLM ATHENS TOKYO MILAN MADRID
PRAGUE WARSAW BUDAPEST AUCKLAND

Recycling programs
for this product may
not exist in your area.

ISBN-13: 978-0-373-71709-5

MITZI'S MARINE

Printed in U.S.A.

ABOUT THE AUTHOR

When an aptitude test labeled her suited for librarian or clergy, Rogenna attempted to shake that good-girl image by joining the U.S. Navy. Ever the rebel, she landed in the chaplain's office, where her duties included operating the base library. Far from being bored, our romantic adventurer served Navy, Coast Guard and Marine Corps personnel as a chaplain's yeoman in such exotic locales as Midway Island and the Pentagon. But even before she shipped off to boot camp, Rogenna worked as a receptionist for the now defunct recruiting station re-created, and somewhat embellished, for this story.

Books by Rogenna Brewer

HARLEQUIN SUPERROMANCE

833—SEAL IT WITH A KISS
980—SIGN, SEAL, DELIVER
1070—MIDWAY BETWEEN YOU AND ME
1223—THE SEAL'S BABY
1478—THE MARINE'S BABY

Don't miss any of our special offers. Write to us at the following address for information on our newest releases.

Harlequin Reader Service
U.S.: 3010 Walden Ave., P.O. Box 1325, Buffalo, NY 14269
Canadian: P.O. Box 609, Fort Erie, Ont. L2A 5X3

For my recruiter, Petty Officer George Sandoval,
Station manager Master Chief Bill Moore
and
Davis Faunce, ENC (Ret)

Because he kept the engraved pen I gave him as I
was leaving for boot camp, then sent it back to me
all these years later for an autograph.
Thanks, Chief, for your quick quips and
answers to my questions.

A special thanks to Annette and her
Marine recruiter husband, Charles, who probably
doesn't remember answering my many
questions all those years ago.

Any mistakes I've made or liberties I've taken
are my own.

To reconnect with shipmates, I look for them
online at
Togetherweserved.com.

CHAPTER ONE

CHIEF PETTY OFFICER Mitzi Zahn entered the store-front Navy/Marine Corps recruiting station. Navy to the left. Marine Corps to the right. The path up the middle was known as the DMZ, demilitarized zone. Potential recruits stepping onto that worn patch of blue carpet were fair game.

For the past several months Mitzi had had the hunting grounds to herself. Which was why the jarhead standing beside her desk, holding the only framed photo to be found there, made her natural territorial instincts kick in.

Letting the heavy glass door swing shut on the sounds of the midweek morning rush, Mitzi cleared her throat. "You must be the new Marine."

Leatherneck looked up, unapologetic.

She couldn't help it—she shivered. Penetrating green eyes, eyes she knew to be hazel when he wasn't decked out in that belted olive drab uniform, gave her service khaki blouse and pants the once-over.

"Mitzi," he said in a timbre that penetrated even deeper than those eyes.

"Calhoun." She caught her breath as she said his name for the first time in over a year—months of devastating loss from which she was just beginning to recover.

"Have I changed that much?" he asked.

She glanced at the photo in his hand and shook her head. "I don't know, maybe," she confessed, her answer running the gambit of her emotions.

Somewhere along the way the man she'd fallen in love with had become a lean, battle-hardened Marine. And even though she'd been there for most of the ten-year transformation, it was as if she was seeing him for the first time.

But he wasn't the only one with battle scars.

"What brings you here, Calhoun?"

The obvious answer was military orders.

He'd left his garrison cap and an official-looking folder on the chair in front of her desk. He was dressed for travel in his service uniform. Sharp military creases in his pants, despite the fact that he'd probably spent hours on an airplane.

"It's good to see you, too," he said in that all-too-familiar tone. "Nice new uniform."

She snatched the picture from him, then set it back down on her desk with deliberate finality. "It's Chief Petty Officer Zahn now," she said, stowing her hat and handbag in the bottom right-hand drawer. The move served to put her behind the gunmetal-gray desk and in the power position.

After all, they were on more than just opposite sides of a piece of government furniture. If he was the new Marine recruiter, then he was her competition.

"Chief," he acknowledged.

Challenge resonated in that single word.

"A chief is the Navy equivalent of a Marine Corps gunnery sergeant," she reminded him. In case he thought that extra stripe on his sleeve meant he outranked her. *"Gunny."*

"For the record, Zahn, I still have date of rank on you." He'd graduated from high school and enlisted in the Marine Corps two years before she'd joined the Navy.

He'd always been at least one pay grade ahead of her. But she'd exceeded all her recruiting quotas, and one of the perks for superior performance was advancement.

"Okay, then…" Just because they were no longer friends didn't mean she wanted to make an enemy of him. "Now that that's settled… Still take your coffee black?"

"Black's fine."

"I like cream and sugar. You'll find the coffee mess and everything you need right over there." She nodded in the general direction of the alcove that led to the back of the building. "Feel free to help yourself," she said, in case her message needed a little reinforcement.

Do not expect me to wait on you.

Waiting on him held a whole other meaning for her.

"Like I said, Chief, can I get you a cup of coffee?"

"Thank you, yes," she responded with a saccharine-sweet smile. She'd make it through today the way she'd made it through any other. By faking it. Turning her attention to the papers piled on her desk, Mitzi struggled to keep her composure.

She'd gotten really good at faking it.

"And Gunny…" She looked up as he started to walk away, noticed the hitch in his step and hesitated. He turned. It was nothing short of a miracle to see him walking again. "Please don't touch anything on my desk," she said, forcing herself not to get caught up in the drama of their shared past. "We have a no-poaching policy in this office."

He stared at her as if she'd been the one caught rifling his desk instead of the other way around. "Isn't it time we called a truce?"

"A truce?"

"We're going to be working together." He gestured toward the empty desk on the opposite side of the room. Just as she'd suspected. He wasn't here for her. Would it have made a difference?

Maybe. Maybe not.

They'd been the best of friends once. More than friends. Now they were…what? Not friends. Not enemies.

He wanted a truce. There was a time when she'd wanted nothing more than to surrender to those hazel-green eyes.

"Bruce Calhoun, Gunnery Sergeant, USMC." He offered his hand. "Marine Corps recruiter, at your service."

She heard the self-reproach behind his words.

For Calhoun there'd be nothing worse than riding out his career behind a desk. For her she'd like nothing better. She'd gotten used to the idea of being home again.

The telephone rang.

Taking a deep breath, Mitzi ignored his outstretched hand and picked up the phone. "Navy Recruiting, Englewood Station. Chief Zahn speaking." She covered the mouthpiece. "Cream and sugar."

CREAM AND SUGAR. As if he needed the reminder.

Dumping two packets into the paper cup, Bruce studied Mitzi while she talked on the telephone. She might not outrank him, but she'd outmaneuvered him.

All of five foot nothing—if he hadn't seen her in action it would've been hard to believe she rescued guys like him for a living.

California. BUD/S training. A lifetime ago. Before Iraq.

Before he'd decided he wasn't worth saving.

If there'd been a spark of something left for him in those columbine-blue eyes, he'd have been here long before now. But there wasn't anything left. Not that he could blame her. He wasn't here to compare her eyes to the state flower.

Bruce scowled at the cup in his hand. He'd reached a new low in his ten-year military career, stirring cream and sugar into coffee with a swizzle stick.

His commanding officer had recommended recruiting school as a way to keep his mind active while his injured body went through the rigors of a long rehabilitation at Balboa—the Naval Medical Center in San Diego.

Recommendations, requests…mere suggestions from a superior were the same as an order to a Marine. And orders were meant to be obeyed without question.

When volun*told,* he did his job—whether that job involved pushing himself to the limit in some war-torn Middle Eastern country or pushing a pencil in his own hometown.

But this was by far his toughest assignment to date. It was clear she didn't want him here any more than he wanted to be here. Did she blame him for her brother's death? As he blamed himself?

The door opened and Bruce looked up to see the United States Army stride in. Tall and fit. Desert cammies and combat boots. The guy looked as if he'd walked off one of those Army recruiting posters next door. He carried a drink tray with two large cups of McDonald's coffee.

Bruce instantly recognized the enemy for who and what he was and put down the coffee he'd been stirring.

"Cream and sugar," Army announced, leaning in for a kiss just as Mitzi hung up the phone.

She pulled back with a quick glance in Bruce's direction. With that less-than-subtle rejection, the other man noticed Bruce tucked into the alcove.

"Didn't see you standing there," he apologized. "You must be the new Marine recruiter." He took two steps in Bruce's direction and held out his hand. "First Sergeant Daniel Estrada, 10th Mountain Division."

Just his luck they were all the same enlisted pay grade. Though Bruce doubted Mitzi had given this guy the same speech she'd given him.

"Calhoun," Bruce said, refusing to meet the other man halfway. "And you must be the *new* boyfriend."

Nice Guy Estrada had already bridged the gap and was in the middle of a firm handshake. He stopped short of an over-the-shoulder double take at the photo on Mitzi's desk and the man he was

shaking hands with as realization dawned. His
smile became tight. Forced. "Nice to meet you,"
Estrada lied smoothly.

"Dan teaches JROTC at the high school."

Bruce grunted in acknowledgment. His own four
years in Junior Reserve Officers Training Corps
had earned him a couple extra stripes out of boot
camp.

"He also coaches the boys' basketball team," she
added after an awkward silence. "Bruce is Keith's
brother," she said to Estrada.

Half brother. But that was neither here nor
there.

They were brothers. They had the same mother,
but Keith's father was Bruce's paternal uncle. Yeah,
a real blended—as in blurred—family.

"Calhoun, of course—I should have realized,"
Estrada said. "Bright kid. Bright future. Couple of
college scouts interested."

"Bruce played basketball in high school," Mitzi
said. She could stop trying to cement a bond. That
was never going to happen.

"Still play?" Estrada asked.

"Not in a long time." Bored by the subject, Bruce
checked his watch. "Excuse me, I was just heading
out for a haircut." He picked up his hat from the
chair and nodded to her on his way to the door.

As if her kissing another man had no effect on
him whatsoever, he added his blessing. "Carry on."

"YOU FORGOT TO MENTION the new Marine was *your* Marine." Dan picked up the photo Bruce had been holding when she walked in.

"He's not *my* Marine." Mitzi took it from him. The picture was of her, her brother and Bruce. "This is the last picture taken of my brother before he was killed."

"I'm sorry," Dan apologized. "Jealousy is one of my less attractive traits. I could make you a list of some of my more positive ones."

She couldn't help but smile, relieved that with Bruce gone, some of the tension she'd been feeling had dissipated.

"For example," he said, perching on the corner of her desk. "I always put the cap back on the toothpaste. And I grew up with three sisters, so I learned early on to put the toilet seat down. Have you made up your mind yet, about Vail?"

They weren't quite at the toothpaste-and-toilet-seat stage of a relationship yet—just a couple casual dates—but she could see herself with him. Dan had asked her to cochaperone a class ski trip in Vail over the Thanksgiving weekend. He owned a cabin there and took his senior class skiing every year.

"Sure, why not?" The kids would be their chaperones as much as they'd be theirs. She saluted him with the cup in her hand. Taking a sip, Mitzi mulled over the need for honesty in a new relationship. She decided on full disclosure in this case.

"He *was* my Marine," she confessed. "I mean, we were engaged. But that's all in the past."

"Okay…" Dan glanced at the snapshot, then back at her. "Just let me know when you're ready to Photoshop him out of the picture." He checked his watch. "I've got a class to teach."

"Danny," Mitzi called as he reached the door. "See you tonight?"

"Of course." Without hesitation he stepped back in to give her a quick kiss before heading out again.

Relieved, Mitzi sank to her seat. Wrapping her hands around the warm paper cup, she stared out the glass front at the slushy, snow-covered street and hoped she hadn't sounded desperate.

Dan had been stopping by on his way to school every morning for weeks. He'd flirted his way to a first date. Then last night she'd taken him to the Broadway Bar & Bowl, where he'd met her father and where she'd laughed for the first time in a long time.

She was ready to date again.

Dan felt safe.

Why did Calhoun have to show up now? And why did she feel this sudden urgency to prove she'd moved on?

Had she moved on?

Just let me know when you're ready to Photoshop him out of the picture.

It had been taken in Kuwait, on one of those rare occasions when the three of them had been in the same place at the same time.

Her brother, Fred Jr.—Freddie to his friends— had joined the Navy right out of high school. Bruce had been born to be a Marine. After joining the Corps, he'd been one of a select group of eighty-six Marines, including five Navy hospital corpsmen serving with the Marine Corps, to train with and integrate into the Navy SEAL teams.

She'd become a rescue swimmer because she couldn't follow them into the SEAL program. But her job gave her an all-access pass into their world.

The guys had just flown in from an op. She had an arm around each of them. Laughing.

Freddie to her right, Bruce to her left and on her left ring finger a sparkling-new diamond ring she was showing off for the camera.

She'd just completed a SAR, search and rescue drill, and earned some well-deserved shore leave when Bruce had hopped out of that helo in the background and walked straight up to her. Without a word they'd kissed and wound up in a dark corner of a military hangar.

Half dressed.

Her back against the wall. Him inside her.

Afterward he'd produced a ring from out of nowhere. She'd socked him in the arm. A gal didn't want to be proposed to while zipping up her flight suit after a quickie.

He'd followed her outside. Got down on bended knee, in front of no less than a hundred witnesses.

"It's about damn time." Freddie had been the first to congratulate them. He'd handed his camera phone to someone and the three of them posed for that picture. Later she and Bruce headed to Dubai for three days and two nights of R & R to celebrate.

Those were the last happy days of her life.

She couldn't just Photoshop Bruce out of the picture without also erasing every memory, good and bad, she was ever going to have of her brother. But Freddie had been the glue that held the three of them together.

Without him something was missing.

CHAPTER TWO

IT WAS A GOOD THING he really didn't need a haircut. There weren't that many good old-fashioned barber shops around anymore, unless you knew where to look. The one he remembered was long gone.

Bruce stood on the corner of Broadway and Hampden, trying to reorient himself by reading the marquee above the Army & Navy Surplus Store. The sign boasted of David Spade buying a jean jacket for a recent *Saturday Night Live* appearance. There was a time when nothing in this town changed except that sign.

Now it all looked different.

Broadway for a few blocks in either direction made up the main drag. One- and two-story turn-of-the-century brick buildings fought for attention among the ongoing revitalization of the area. To the north was Denver and to the south, the tech centers and sprawling suburbs. Both threatened to swallow Englewood whole.

"You Mitzi's Marine?"

Bruce realized he'd been standing, lost in his thoughts, in the middle of the sidewalk, and he started to move closer to the intersection.

"Hey, I'm talking to you," a wheelchair-bound man insisted, wheeling after him. "You hear me? Or that grenade take out your hearing, too?"

"I heard you," Bruce answered, not bothering to hide his irritation. He didn't make eye contact, either. He'd spotted the beggar from across the street.

"Hallelujah—he's not deaf, just a dumb-ass Marine. Knock on wood."

Bruce sidestepped the wheelie's attempt to knock on his prosthetic leg. Which was *not* made of wood.

"I knew you was a gimp a mile down the road," the old-timer boasted.

Bruce bristled at the use of the term *gimp*. He took pride in being able to walk without a limp. Stairs used to give him away. But with the aid of modern technology and practice—months and months of practice—he'd perfected his stride. As an above-the-knee amputee, he'd had to relearn to walk using his hips to propel himself forward, rather than his legs.

"Pride goeth before a fall, spitshine," the old-timer said. "Least, that's what they tell me down at the Salvation Army."

The light on the corner flashed Walk and Bruce hurried across the street, with the wheelie keeping pace. "Spare change for a fellow Marine down on his luck?"

If he'd been wearing a different uniform, Bruce had no doubt the old-timer would have been Army, Navy, Air Force or whatever branch of service suited his purpose.

Marines did not beg on street corners. At least not those with a shred of self-respect.

"You know that homeless-vet act went out with the seventies."

"Been on these streets since Nam," the so-called vet insisted.

"I don't doubt it," Bruce said, picking up his pace.

"You think you're better than me, son? You and me, we ain't so different."

Bruce stopped in his tracks. "First of all, I'm not your *son*," he said, turning on the old man. But that meant he had to look at him, really look at him.

Greasy shoulder-length comb-over. A patch over his right eye. And a weathered face as wrinkled as one of Aunt Dottie's dried-apple dolls. He smelled like the bottom of a cider barrel. Piss and vinegar. But a strong wind would blow the old fart away, he was so thin.

The vet's military field jacket was tattered and worn, but offered some protection against the slushy gray November morning. More disturbing was the prosthetic leg sticking foot-up out of the junk packed on the back of the wheelchair.

The old-timer was missing his right leg from above the knee down—a mirror-image injury to Bruce's own missing left leg. A RAK, right-leg-above-the-knee amputee. And a LAK, left-leg-above-the-knee amputee.

Bruce felt the familiar sinking sensation in his gut as he dug out his wallet. He'd been in prime physical condition before being cut down. He could have gone soft in the hospital, let the pain and the loss drive him to suicide like Stuart, or to bitterness like Hatch.

But he hadn't. He hadn't because there was nothing more important than getting back to his unit.

Unit, Corps, God and country.

Every Marine knew the order of things.

It was the one thing that kept him going.

But this guy...*this guy* was right out of Bruce's waking nightmare. He had to have been young once. One quirk of fate and thirty years from now Bruce could be an old wheelie on a street corner, trying to live off a substandard disability check and begging for change.

"Here." He shoved a dollar bill at the guy. Feeling the urge to put as much distance as possible between him and the wheelie, he continued up the block.

"A buck?" The next light turned green as he reached the corner, and the wheelchair-bound vet followed Bruce into another crosswalk. He wasn't using his hands to operate the chair. He kept pace by scooting along with his single foot, maneuvering from one dip in the curb to the other. "Do you have any idea how much public transportation costs these days? How am I supposed to get to the VA on a buck?"

"How much?" Bruce demanded, coming to an abrupt halt. He didn't for one minute believe the old-timer was headed to the Veterans Administration.

"Four dollars to get me there and back. Another couple dollars to fill my belly…"

"Here's a five." Bruce shoved it at him. Kissing that six bucks goodbye, he started walking again.

"Them damn drivers don't make change." The old-timer kept pace with him, grumbling.

"How much to get you to stop following me?" Bruce demanded, losing all patience with the old guy.

"Depends on where you're headed."

"Right here. This is where I'm headed," Bruce said, walking up to the recruiting office door with the Navy and Marine Corps logos and opening it wide.

The two-story brick-and-mortar office had received a recent face-lift. The sign above the two doors read "Armed Forces Recruiting Station."

"Well, hell, son, that's where I'm headed, too." He blew past Bruce. "I asked was you Mitzi's Marine?"

"I'm not Mitzi's anything!" Bruce said a little too vehemently.

"MITZI!" the old-timer called out. "You here?"

"Be right out, Henry," she answered from somewhere beyond the alcove. The bathroom? The storage room? The stairs to the second-story loft, maybe?

The Navy/Marine Corps half of the recruiting station was divided into front offices and back offices, separated by a short hallway. Alcoves built into either side of the hall were fitted with kitchen-style counters and cabinets.

With Bruce hot on his wheels, the old-timer scooted off in search of her. "Hey! You can't go back there."

The one-eyed wheelie scowled at him. "Says who?"

"Says me!" Bruce was about to argue further when Mitzi stepped out from the unisex bathroom in the locker area. Were those tears she was trying to hide? He felt a familiar tightness in his chest.

The last time he'd seen her cry she was running from his hospital room.

"Henry Dawson Meyers," she said, "what is that thing over your eye?"

"Found it in a Dumpster," Henry said proudly. "Lots of good stuff left over from Halloween."

"What have I told you about digging through Dumpsters?"

The guy had the decency to blush. Mitzi took the eye patch from him and stepped back into the open bathroom. After washing the patch with soap and water, she wiped it down with a paper towel and handed it back to Henry, who tucked the prop into his jacket pocket.

Bruce stood there shaking his head. "Ol' Henry here has a bus to catch," he said. He'd put the guy in a position where he'd have to leave or be caught in a lie.

"Oh? You don't want a ride today?" Mitzi asked Henry.

"Course I do." Henry glared at Bruce with two weathered eyes.

"I give Henry a ride to the VA hospital every Wednesday," Mitzi explained.

"Of course you do." First he'd been outmaneuvered by Mitzi, aka mini-Marine. Then a one-legged con man with a fake eye patch had tried to take him for a ride. Not today. "I'll drive," Bruce insisted.

MITZI BEGAN DIGGING through the glove compartment of his government vehicle. "What are you doing?" Bruce demanded.

"Looking for this," she said, hanging the handicap permit from the rearview mirror.

Bruce yanked it down and shoved it back into the box. "We're just dropping him off," he said, pulling up to the front entrance of the VA hospital.

"You don't want to stop in and say hi to your mother?" she asked, incredulous. "What about your aunt? You probably haven't seen her in ages."

"I saw my mother at breakfast." His mother and paternal aunt were registered nurses. Both worked at the VA after having served in Vietnam together thirtysome-odd years ago. That's where Aunt Dottie had introduced his mom to his dad and his uncle John.

True, he hadn't seen Aunt Dottie in a while. But he'd had enough well-intentioned smothering for his first day home. His mother had fussed over him at breakfast more than when he'd been an inpatient at Balboa.

Hospitals weren't exactly on his list of favorite places, no matter who worked where and what shift. Not after his extended stay. Been there, done that. Didn't need the handicap permit to prove it.

Bruce put a hand to his collar to loosen the choke hold his tie had on him. "Even if I *was* sticking around," he said, "I wouldn't need to take up a handicap parking place."

"I just thought you might want the extra room for Henry's wheelchair."

"That's why there's a loading zone."

"Get me out of here," Henry demanded from the backseat. "I've had about all I can stand of the Bickersons. If I'd of known you two was gonna fight the whole way I woulda taken my chances with the bus."

Bruce and Mitzi exchanged censuring looks.

He managed not to slam anything as he got out of the car, got the wheelchair from the trunk and pulled it alongside Henry's open door. The old-timer barely had the upper-body strength to transfer himself into the chair. Once he did, Bruce shut the car door and wheeled Henry over to the dip in the curb.

"I can take it from here," Mitzi insisted.

Bruce eased off the handles. "You're going in?"

"You can wait in the car in the farthest spot in the parking lot, for all I care. But I have business inside and you're the one who insisted on driving."

"How long do you think you'll be?"

She shrugged. "Half hour maybe."

"That long?"

"Just go, Calhoun. I'll find a ride back to the station." Pushing Henry's wheelchair toward the sliding double doors, Mitzi left Bruce standing on the curb.

"I like the other fella better," Henry was saying as the automatic doors slid open.

"Wait!" Bruce stopped her before she could push through to the lobby. "Here," he said, removing the spare key from his key ring. "Keep the car. I'll walk back to the station."

"You can't walk all the—"

"Then I guess I'll have to run," he said, squaring his shoulders.

"That's not what I meant."

"Yeah, I know what you meant, Chief. I'll park the car in a handicap spot where you'll be sure to find it."

She expected him to fall on his ass.

Maybe he would, but he'd be damned if he was going to fail without trying. He'd never give up the fight, no matter how low she set her expectations.

Eighteen months earlier
Baghdad, Iraq

"Hurry up, you lazy son of a gun," Freddie taunted as Bruce and his charge ran behind the truck, trying to catch up to the slow-moving vehicle.

Bruce threw his weapon over the tailgate. Hopping onto the back bumper, he reached behind to help the new kid up and over. Lieutenant Luke Calhoun slid down to make room for them. Bruce declined with a shake of his head.

Stepping over first Luke's, then Freddie's outstretched legs, Bruce acknowledged Alpha and Bravo squads with a nod. The six men on the opposite bench were all Navy SEALs. While his side, a combo of Recon Marines and Navy SEALs, grumbled about having to make room for seven, the truck could hold twice as many in a pinch.

"Move your ass over, Freddie," Bruce said, squeezing himself and the new kid into the middle of the bench seat to the left of Freddie. There was nowhere he'd rather be than right here. This was his home and these guys were his family.

Luke literally. And Freddie soon to be.

"Gum?" Freddie offered.

"Thanks." Bruce pocketed it for later.

Taking a moment to catch his breath after almost missing his ride, Bruce leaned back against the canvas cover of the supply truck and closed his eyes. Not only was he late getting back, he'd been put in charge of their newest team member, a young hospital corpsman by the name of Manuel Henriquez.

"Jeez, wipe that grin off your face or I will," Freddie threatened.

"Can't," Bruce said, his grin the only thing visible beneath the brim of his helmet.

"You just spent three days in Dubai with my sister. Humor me," Freddie insisted.

"Never even left the hotel room."

"Too much information, bro." Freddie elbowed him in the gut, hard. "You're not married to her yet."

"O-kay." Bruce let out his battered breath. "I deserved that. But I'm still smiling." He tugged his brim lower so Freddie wouldn't have to see the satisfied smile on his face.

"Just make sure she's the one still smiling or I'm going to kick your ass from here to Timbuktu."

"Where's Timbuktu?" Henriquez asked.

"West Africa, Mali," Luke answered, around Freddie. Luke was a college grad, an officer, and as such the lieutenant in charge of the operation.

A really smart guy. Imagine coming halfway around the world to discover that about your own brother. Half brother. They had the same father—not that Bruce held that against Luke.

Bruce peeked out from under his helmet at Freddie. "You think you can kick my ass all the way to West Africa? I'd like to see you try."

"How far is not the point. The point is I can, and I will," Freddie boasted. "Mitzi loves you," he said in all seriousness.

Bruce shoved his helmet back. "I know."

"This isn't high school. You don't get to break her heart again. Not and have me as a friend. Marriage is for real. You hurt her..."

"I'm not going to pretend we have it all figured out. With her there and me here it's going to be tough." They were having to shout above the grinding gears of the diesel engine, making this conversation a little less private and a lot more uncomfortable than Bruce would have wanted. "We love each other. We'll find a way to make it work."

"Why now?"

"Why not now?"

"In case you haven't noticed, we're in the middle of a war zone. Chances are you'll make my baby sister a widow before your first anniversary."

"Thanks for that optimism."

Freddie's family had moved next door to Bruce's when they were both eight. They'd been best friends ever since. Bruce's relationship with his best friend's little sister was a lot more complicated.

They'd been on again/off again since high school. Being in two different branches of military service didn't make it easy to be together. But in high school she'd been his first love. His only love.

And he'd been hers.

She wasn't the only woman he'd been with since then. Just the only one who mattered. When they were together they were inseparable. And when they were apart?

Well, he used to drive himself crazy thinking about it. Finally he drove himself crazy enough to propose.

Before Kuwait it had been eight months since he'd last seen her. Eight very long months. He'd been reading between the lines of her emails. There was this guy, her crew chief. Nothing serious as far as he could tell. Just the way she dropped his name every now and again left Bruce thinking.

And thinking was dangerous.

"I don't want to lose her."

"Fear is not a reason to get married."

"Reason enough."

"Couldn't you have said you knocked her up? I could respect that, at least."

It was Bruce's turn to elbow his future brother-in-law in the gut. "Mitzi's not pregnant."

"Too bad. I was kind of hoping you'd take her away from all this." Freddie spread his arms to encompass the thirteen of them sweating it out in the oppressive heat of the truck's interior.

The thought had crossed his mind. But Mitzi wouldn't have gone along with that and he was far more afraid of her kicking his ass than of her brother's threats. "We've agreed—"

"Don't wait too long to make me an uncle."
No kids.

DRESS SHOES WEREN'T MADE for running. But Bruce managed the distance without a serious slip. Thanks to his new all-terrain leg, he could push himself further than before. Pavement gave way to gravel and he didn't miss a beat. Slowing to a stop, Bruce propped himself against the metal fire door at the back of the recruiting station to catch his breath.

There were days like today when he felt unworthy of the uniform. He loosened his tie and dragged it through the collar. As if he'd let everyone he cared about down.

The sock on his right foot was soaked through from the melting snow. His left foot, too—he just couldn't feel it. But his stump throbbed a constant reminder of all that had changed. Eyes closed, he let the sensation take him back to Iraq. He'd been about to say *No kids.*

Or maybe he'd said *No kids.* He couldn't remember.

How tragic if those were his last words to Freddie.

Don't wait too long to make me an uncle.

The RPG had ripped through the truck then.

If Bruce had sat on the end...

What if? What if he'd been two minutes earlier?

Two minutes later? Missed the transport altogether? Sat next to Luke? Instead he'd pushed Luke and Freddie to one side and hogged the middle.

And his brother and his best friend were dead.

CHAPTER THREE

BY THE TIME MITZI RETURNED to the office, Calhoun had showered and changed into combat utilities. She tucked her hat and handbag back into the bottom drawer, along with the prescription of birth control she'd picked up at the VA, and settled in at her desk.

She didn't know if he could still run a five-minute mile, but she knew the word *can't* was not in his vocabulary.

Unfortunately that stubborn streak extended to his personal relationships, as well. Come mid-afternoon she wanted to scream at him out of frustration. She'd never quite understood the term *deafening silence* until now. Everything left unsaid over the past eighteen months lingered in the air like the half-eaten egg salad sandwich she'd tossed out at lunch.

If they were going to work together they'd have to learn to communicate again. She'd been wrong to reject his offer of a truce.

But she'd be damned if she'd tell him that.

"School's out," she said with a nod toward the pedestrian traffic outside. Within minutes two girls, trying to look much older than their seventeen or eighteen years, walked through the door.

The pair stopped in front of Bruce's desk while he continued to do whatever it was he was doing at his computer. Mitzi was pretty sure his emails to his old command had little to do with recruiting.

"May I help you?" he asked after a while.

"Hi." Swallowed up by an oversize varsity letterman's jacket, the first to speak wore a cheer skirt and cropped top underneath. Mitzi didn't know her name, but the other girl was Kelly Casey. Kelly had on jeans and layered T-shirts. She carried drumsticks and hid behind her schoolbooks.

Mitzi could relate to the band geek. She'd been one. As well as captain of the swim team. What she'd never been was a cheerleader. Or a blonde.

She'd never seen the two together before. They made an odd pair.

"Hi, Heather," Bruce responded without inflection.

Heather took that as an invitation to perch on his desk and Mitzi got a glimpse of the name on the back of the jacket. *Calhoun.*

So that's how they knew each other.

Heather must be Keith's girlfriend.

"So are you, like, a Marine?" Heather picked

up Bruce's stapler and played with it until he took it from her and set it out of her reach.

"I *am* a Marine."

"Did you, like, fight in the war or whatever?"

"Whatever," he agreed. Calhoun stood up so that he towered over the two girls. "Excuse me, ladies. I'm busy right now."

Heather shrugged. *Whatever.*

Kelly followed her to the door before turning around. "Will you tell Keith we were here?" Her cheeks, already pink from the winterlike weather outside, brightened. "And that I can't tutor him this Saturday. I have to work."

Calhoun offered a curt nod. Mitzi frowned after the departing pair, then at him.

"What?" he demanded.

"Whatever." She shrugged. "Be careful."

"Of those two?"

"The last recruiter is gone because he gave in to temptation. Seventeen may be legal in this state, but there's a very fine line—"

"You know me better than that."

"It's not you I'm worried about." That uniform and all that brooding silence could be hard for a young girl to resist. Mitzi propped herself against his desk and picked up his stapler. "Don't you re-member what it was like to be seventeen?"

At seventeen he'd been her whole world.

"No," he denied, taking the stapler from her.

The brush of his hand took her by surprise. Every scarred knuckle, every callus on his palm were as familiar to her as the memory of his touch.

"Me, either," she lied. Heaven help her, she wasn't seventeen anymore and it was hard for *her* to resist.

Lest she forget, when she was twenty-four he'd brought that world crashing down.

She crossed the room and picked up the folder with his travel orders. "Here," she said, handing it to him. "You left this on a chair and it wound up on my desk."

"Sorry about that."

"Not a problem," she said, heading back to her desk.

"Did you read them?" He sounded curious, not angry.

His curiosity intrigued her. "Your orders are none of my business, Gunny."

"I just thought you should know I'm only here temporarily."

It sounded like a warning not to get her hopes up. She knew better. "I guessed as much."

"Once my detachment gets back to The Boathouse, I'll be joining them. I'll have to pass a physical fitness test first. But as soon as they call…" He shrugged.

He'd be gone. Back in the line of fire.

Not a matter of if, but when.

The Boathouse was a modern space-aged building tucked into the boat basin at Camp Pendleton in San Diego. If his recon unit wasn't there they could be almost anywhere.

Which was obviously where he wanted to be.

Anywhere but here.

"It's what you wanted." Was it petty of her not to be happy for him? Even if he got himself killed just to prove he was worthy of being called a Marine?

"Hey," Keith called out, coming through the door, basketball tucked under his arm. "I hear there's a new Marine Corps recruiter in town. Where do I sign?"

"Over my dead body," Bruce declared.

"I'm serious." Keith approached the desk and Mitzi retreated to her side of the room.

"So am I." Bruce stood with his hands on his hips. A dozen cold calls his first day down the list of high school seniors and not a single lead, then in walks his eighteen-year-old brother ready to sign on the dotted line.

As if he was ever going to let that happen.

Keith dropped into the chair opposite Bruce's desk, put his basketball and backpack at his feet. "Seriously," he said, kicking back, with his size thirteens up on Bruce's desk. "I want to join the Corps."

"Seriously." Bruce knocked Keith's feet to the

floor, then sat where they'd been. "You're going to college."

"College is an expensive waste of time."

"Coach says your scholarship prospects are good."

"Yeah, so?"

"So you're going."

"You didn't."

Bruce crossed his arms. "And look where it got me."

"I don't see what's so bad about being you."

"Then you're not looking hard enough."

"It's family tradition. You—"

"Didn't have the same opportunities you have. And sure as hell didn't have your grades. You're a smart kid—act like it."

"I'm sick of school." Keith pushed to his feet, full of restless energy. They were roughly the same height now. When had the kid shot up those last few inches? "I'm sick and tired of people telling me what I can and can't do."

"And you want to be a Marine? You're going to have someone in your face 24/7 telling you when to eat, sleep, drink and take a piss. Hoorah!"

"That's just boot camp."

"What's that poster behind me say?"

Keith tilted his head to see around him. "Every Marine a rifleman."

"Deer hunting. Few years back. Me, you, *your*

dad." Despite the fact that Uncle John had been more of a father to him than Big Luke, Bruce couldn't bring himself to call his uncle and step-father *Dad,* so he settled for John. Or *your dad* when talking to Keith. "You stared down that three-point buck, but couldn't bring yourself to shoot."

"I was thirteen."

"Fifteen."

"It was my first time hunting. And I don't like venison all that much either," he added for good measure.

"You been hunting since? To a rifle range?"

"No," Keith admitted. "But I know how to shoot and I know I'll get the training I need in boot camp."

"Go home," Bruce said.

"So I'm not you. There are other jobs in the Marine Corps besides Force Recon."

Bruce had been Recon, parachute and diver qualified when he'd gone through BUD/S train-ing and integrated into Navy SEALs. He'd added recruiter to his list. And if he was any kind of a recruiter he'd be showing Keith his options right now.

But this was his brother and there was no way in hell he was going to put the kid in harm's way. Just because Keith knew how to fire a weapon didn't mean he knew jack about war.

"Like what, admin?" Bruce asked. "Think you're going to sit behind a desk all day until your ass is as wide as the chair? No matter what your military occupational specialty, you're going to fight. That's what a Marine does."

Unless you're a recruiter stuck behind a desk.

"Maybe not admin," Keith agreed. "But there are some pretty cool jobs in the Marine Corps."

"Like…?" Bruce prompted.

"Cameraman. I took a photography class last year. I'm pretty good at it." The kid had done his homework.

But it was Bruce's job to know all eighty of the Marine Corps occupational fields. He reached for a thick three-ring binder and opened it to "Combat Camera." "What do all of these jobs have in common? Combat illustrator," he read. "Combat lithographer. Combat photographer. Combat videographer. Could it be the word *combat?*" he practically shouted. "Besides which—" he slammed the book shut "—I don't have an opening for a cameraman. That's CNN's job these days."

"I'm not a kid anymore. I'm eighteen. I don't need your permission. I could walk into any recruiting office in the state and enlist," Keith threatened.

"Try it and I'll kick your ass from here to Timbuktu."

"What the hell, Bruce? I came to you. You're my brother. You're supposed to help me!"

Bruce could understand being sick of school. Sick and tired of being told what to do. At eighteen Keith was well on his way to becoming a man. What he couldn't understand was his brother turning his back on a chance to play basketball for four more years.

That didn't make sense.

"I'm *trying* to help you." Frustration tinged Bruce's voice. "Trust me. I know you well enough to know you're not cut out for the Marine Corps."

He didn't even realize he and his brother stood toe-to-toe until Mitzi put a gentle but firm hand on each of them. "You're scaring my DEPers."

Keith slunk back to his seat. And Bruce sat back on his desk. The front office was full, every couch, every chair occupied. When had that happened? Three guys and one gal. DEPers, kids on the delayed entry program, enlisted while still in high school for guaranteed jobs after graduation.

Mitzi handed him and his brother a can of soda, presumably to cool them off. Bruce popped the top. "What's this I hear about you needing a tutor?"

"So you're just going to change the subject?" Keith accused, tapping his can before opening it.

"Skinny, dark-haired girl. Lives around the corner from us." Bruce held his ground.

His brother wavered under his steady scrutiny.

"Kelly Casey. I help her with math, she helps me with Spanish."

"Since when do you need help with Spanish?"

With Bruce on the offense, Keith became defensive. "Since...*whenever*."

"Mom mentioned your grades were slipping."

"One lousy B on a calculus test."

More than one, according to their mother. "You're better than that," Bruce said. "And by the way, Heather stopped by today."

"So?" Keith took a big gulp of pop and hid whatever it was he felt for Heather behind a shrug.

Was Heather the reason for Keith's general lack of interest in continuing education? Did he think he was going to marry her? Live happily ever after?

Bruce glanced over at Mitzi, involved in discussion with her DEPers. It looked as if they were getting ready for physical training. She'd changed into gray sweatpants. Dark blue letters spelled out Navy down one leg. She wore a snug gray T-shirt that showed off the athletic lines of her body from her slender neck to her slim wrists.

He could circle those wrists with one hand. Band them like steel. Hold them above her head. Kiss all the hollows of her neck. She'd put up a fight at first because she hated giving up control.

She glanced back, caught him drooling over her breasts and signaled her displeasure with the tilt of her chin. Then she gathered her crew and headed outside.

Bruce watched her all the way out the door. His self-imposed abstinence had gone on too long. Eighteen months too long. He hadn't gone that long since… He'd never gone that long.

Did Estrada know the secrets to her surrender?

Would the schoolteacher be the one snuggling up next to her for the rest of his life? Bruce could have had that lifetime commitment. Before his injury it had seemed that clear. After, all muddled.

But no one married their high school sweetheart.

Least of all a Marine.

"Girls can cloud a guy's judgment," he continued. "Maybe you and Heather should think about taking a break for a while. At least until after graduation." He knew firsthand that *break* meant break up. "And I don't want your girlfriend and her friends hanging around the office anymore, either."

"Heather's not my girlfriend," Keith said. "We haven't dated since eighth grade."

Eighth grade? The kid was dating in eighth grade?

Bruce hadn't started dating until… Okay, Mitzi had been in ninth grade, but he'd been in eleventh—a junior. It took a lot of restraint for a guy to wait that long for a girl. The wait had been worth it, though.

Definitely worth it at the time.

"She was wearing your jacket," Bruce pointed out. He didn't know what they called it these days—dating, not dating, hooking up. But back in his day, a guy gave up his letterman jacket for only one of two reasons. He was getting laid. Or he wanted to get laid. "Are you sleeping with Heather? And her friend? Because that's just asking for trouble."

Keith pushed to his feet again, fists balled. "What business is it of yours anyway?"

Bruce was back on his feet, too. "You damn well better be using a condom. *Every* time," he warned. "You have your whole life ahead of you. Don't screw it up!"

Keith snatched his backpack. "Who are you to give me relationship advice? Your fiancée is dating my coach!" He took an envelope out of his backpack and placed it on Mitzi's desk. "Invitation to Career Day. You don't get one."

Bruce picked up Keith's forgotten basketball from under the chair. He called to his brother just as Keith reached the door. "Hey!"

Keith caught it in one Calhoun-sized hand. If Bruce had anything to say about it, his brother would play college ball.

Heather walked in carrying Keith's letterman jacket.

She waved to Bruce. "Hiya."

Bruce offered a halfhearted wave.

To Keith she said, "You left your jacket at Kelly's again." Not so sweetly.

"I told you, I gave it to her. Hers got stolen at band practice. She doesn't have the money to buy a new one. And it's starting to get cold."

Heather rolled her pretty brown eyes. "I'll find her a hoodie or something of mine to wear." She parted with Keith's jacket grudgingly. She might not want the other girl to have it, but that didn't mean she didn't want it for herself. "Kelly can't meet up with you on Saturday. She volunteered to pass out books at the VA hospital again. I don't see how being a candy stripper is supposed to make her a better doctor."

Had Heather just said candy *stripper?*

Not the brightest bulb in the box. Not the dimmest, either. Her comment seemed calculated.

"Actually," Bruce couldn't help but point out, "volunteering is a good way to see if you're cut out for something." To Keith he said, "I'm going to start putting my DEPers through their paces next week." Did he even have any DEPers?

Keith accepted the challenge. "I'll be there."

CHAPTER FOUR

"BE WHERE?" Mitzi asked, coming in on the tail end of their conversation. Keith and Heather were already on their way out the door.

"Do I have any DEPers?" Bruce asked.

"Don't think so." She twisted the cap off her water bottle. "All your kids were absorbed into other stations when the last recruiter left several months ago."

He sized up the kids lined up at the minifridge. "Mind if I borrow a couple of yours?"

"Knock yourself out." Sipping water, Mitzi looked fresh as a flower. Her kids looked a lot more wilted.

"How far did you run them?" He started unbuttoning his uniform shirt. His hands stalled in the process. Was she checking him out?

More likely inventorying his body parts.

"'Bout a mile."

He looked over at the kids in question.

"A twelve-minute mile," she said defensively.

"I'm not trying to kill them before they get to boot camp."

Slow. Even for a *Navy* mile.

The average recruit didn't have to run much faster than that. And he'd never met anyone who could outrun a bullet.

"How many Navy SEAL recruits?" he asked the kids directly. Two of the boys raised their hands. Both looked reasonably fit. "A ten- or twelve-minute mile isn't going to cut it. SEALs have a sixty percent attrition rate. Think you could run another couple miles for me today?"

Both boys nodded eagerly.

"Any hospital corpsmen?" he asked, looking to the third guy in the group. These were just a couple Navy rates he knew that were the most likely to see some action with their Marine brethren. The kid avoided eye contact.

The girl raised her hand. Chances were she wasn't going to be assigned to a Marine Corps combat unit. Then again, she might. The days of G.I. Jane were here.

Both the Army and the Marine Corps were finding ways around the "noncombatant" rules for women.

Case in point, Mitzi. A five-foot-nothing Navy rescue swimmer who could haul his six-foot-plus ass out of the water.

He nodded the girl toward the SEAL twins. She beamed at him as she followed the boys outside.

"What's your rate? Navy job," he clarified for the kid, who looked as if he'd sat on the sidelines most of his life.

A gamer? A little chunky. A little nerdy.

The glasses didn't help. And he'd probably gotten in under a weight waiver—which meant he would have to lose a few pounds before he shipped out anyway. But Bruce wasn't going to embarrass the kid by saying so. He'd just work it off him.

"Aviation electronics," the boy answered.

"Get out there with the rest of 'em, brainiac. If you'd said nuclear field I might have given you a pass."

Not. Every geek and gearhead had to get through boot camp before operating those nuclear-powered ships and subs.

"You coming?" Bruce asked Mitzi as he stripped down to his olive-green T-shirt, hanging his shirt on the back of his chair. Now she wouldn't even look at him.

"I'll pass." She picked up the invitation Keith had left on her desk. "Career Day? Are you going?"

"I'm not invited."

"I take it the conversation with your brother didn't end well."

"I think he's sneaking around with the brunette behind Heather's back." He just didn't know why.

If, as his brother had said, Keith and Heather hadn't dated since eighth grade, why all the secrecy?

"Kelly," Mitzi said, remembering the girl's name when he didn't. "The one who hides behind her books? She's one of my Officer Candidate School referrals. The Navy's going to pay her way through college and med school."

"The candy striper who wants to be a Navy doctor," he said, cementing Kelly in his brain as something other than the brunette with the rockin' *seventeen-year-old* body.

"She's a nice girl."

"It's the nice ones a guy has to watch out for."

Mitzi crossed her arms and stepped across the DMZ, their own little no-man's-land that separated the Navy from the Marines. "I was a nice girl. Are you accusing me of something, Calhoun? Like ruining your nonexistent basketball career?"

Harsh even for a reality check. "Not a chance, Chief."

"Don't confuse what you *think* you wanted at Keith's age with what you really wanted. I was there when you turned down those basketball scholarships to join the Marine Corps, remember?"

"Fair enough." In high school he'd been a big fish in a small pond with little chance of reaching his Final Four dreams. He knew it. Even back then. Especially when only the smallest junior colleges had even bothered to look him over. Basketball was never the be-all and end-all for him. For him the Corps was his calling. He didn't see that in Keith. "I'd just hate for him to give up his dreams so young."

"You have to let him make his own mistakes."

"You seen him play?" he asked. He had on rare occasions, in years past when his brother first made the varsity team as a freshman. Mostly he'd heard secondhand accounts from his family.

"A couple times," she admitted without further comment. Which he assumed meant those couple of times had been since she'd started dating the boy's basketball coach. "Bruce." She hesitated. He watched a range of emotions cross her face. "Lock up when you leave, please. I have a…date tonight."

Ouch.

Your fiancée is dating my coach.

Ex-fiancée.

Bruce felt a surge of jealousy unlike anything he'd experienced since high school. And he'd been jealous plenty since then.

One problem.

He no longer had the right to be jealous.

AFTER WORK BRUCE SPENT about an hour and a half at the gym. The PT he'd inflicted on the Navy DEPers was nothing compared to his own physical fitness routine. He worked hard to stay fit. Prosthetics were expensive.

A residual limb could change over the course of a lifetime. It was important for him to maintain his weight to within five pounds. And to stay active to keep his thigh muscles—his stump—from atrophying.

Outside the gym Bruce zipped up his sweat jacket and cut through the parking lot.

He didn't own a car—he'd sold it predeployment.

Afterward he hadn't seen the point of owning one until he was back on his feet. Then once he was back on his feet his sole purpose had been to redeploy, so again, what was the point? In San Diego he'd had plenty of buddies when he wanted to hitch a ride, and here he had family and the use of two government vehicles—a nondescript sedan and a pimped-out Hummer.

So even though there was a chill to the night air, he preferred to walk. Because it was good exercise. And because he could. Walking was something he'd never take for granted again.

On his way home he grabbed a sandwich from the Spicy Pickle across from the recruiting station. He'd locked up as instructed. The storefront was dark—not that he'd expected Mitzi to be there at this hour, just that he wondered where she was spending her nights these days.

Had she moved back home with her father? Found a place of her own? There were several new apartment complexes in the vicinity. Was she living in one of them?

Or was she spending her nights with Estrada?

At this very moment Army/Navy could be snuggled up on the couch, fighting over the remote and discussing plans to move in together. Maybe they were already living together.

At the end of the block Bruce cut through the alley. It was darker and suited his mood. Henry was there digging through a trash can behind an Italian restaurant.

"Thought she told you to quit Dumpster diving."

"A man's gotta eat."

"Ever heard of a soup kitchen?"

The old-timer made a sour face. "They make me pray for my supper. Out here I don't have to pretend to be grateful to nobody. 'Sides—" he dug out a half-eaten piece of crusty garlic bread and took a bite "—food's better." He offered Bruce a piece.

Bruce shook his head. Although he'd scavenged for meals out of trash cans in BUD/S training, he'd never had to put that training to the test. And hoped he never would.

"Here," he said without thinking. He opened his Spicy Pickle bag and dug out his sandwich, offering half of his gobbler panini to Henry along with a napkin.

The old-timer looked at him suspiciously. "You're not going to make me pray?"

"No," Bruce said. "Haven't been doing a lot of that myself lately."

Henry snorted, but took the offering. Bruce sat on an upturned dented metal trash can and bit into the turkey-and-feta sandwich. "How'd it go at the VA?" he asked.

"Could ask you the same thing," Henry countered.

It was Bruce's turn to snort.

"Sounds about right," Henry said. "What the hell kind of cheese is this?" He spat out his first bite. Then he opened his sandwich and picked off the cheese before taking a second. "Can I get that pickle from you?"

Ol' Henry sure wasn't shy about asking for what he wanted. Or, for that matter, making it clear when he didn't want something. Bruce gave up the pickle and the chips, then finished off his half of the panini.

Feta wasn't his favorite cheese, either. A little salty for his taste. After brushing off his crumbs, Bruce crumpled the empty sack and tossed it, for a three-point shot, into the Dumpster across the alley.

"Night," he said. Somehow *good* night didn't

seem appropriate to the situation. He didn't ask if Henry had a place to stay. He was afraid he knew the answer, and asking the question would somehow make him responsible. If the old man didn't have enough sense to get in out of the cold, that was his problem. "You're going to be all right tonight? Got enough blankets?"

Damn it. He really hadn't meant to ask.

"Got everything I need," Henry said, letting him off the hook.

"Good," Bruce said, then got the hell out of there before Henry could think of something he really needed. Like a roof over his head.

You and me, we ain't so different.

Henry was right, of course. Bruce didn't own a car. Or a home. Or have someone to share his life with. He'd pushed her away for this chance to get back to his unit.

His best friend, his half brother and his leg had been taken from him. All his buddies were in and around San Diego, or deployed overseas.

He had a desk job he couldn't stand after one day. And the recon job he loved was still out of reach. At least until he passed the obstacle course.

Soon.

Meanwhile, he did have the one thing Henry didn't have. Family.

The house was empty when he got there.

He found a sticky note tacked to the refrigerator door—"7:00 p.m."

That could have meant almost anything. But in the Calhoun household it meant there was a basketball game tonight. Why hadn't his mother mentioned it at breakfast? Why hadn't Keith said something this afternoon?

He more or less knew the answer to that one.

It was a quarter to seven now. He didn't have time to shower or change if he wanted to make the first quarter. He looked down at his sweats. No big deal.

Pocketing the house keys, he walked the few blocks to Englewood High School. The parking lot was near capacity and he was glad he wasn't trolling for a space. Light spilled from the building. Every time the doors opened he could hear the band pumping up the crowd.

Once inside, he found the sound almost deafening.

The halls outside the gym smelled of buttered popcorn and were lined with tables of blue-and-white team T-shirts with EHS printed on them. Both were being sold to raise money for the team. He bought a bag of the popcorn and entered the gym.

The Englewood Pirates bleachers were full.

He didn't bother searching for his family. They'd find each other eventually. Instead he made his way to the nearest available seat. Which happened to be fifteen frustrating rows up in the opposing team's territory—The Alameda Pirates. Both teams were Pirates.

This was the rivalry of the year—the battle for Pirates' pride.

At least he didn't stand out as the only Pirates fan sitting on the wrong side. He wore nondescript gray sweats and there was plenty of blue and white filling in around him—both teams' colors were blue and white.

He caught Keith's attention from the bench, and they nodded to each other. Home team was wearing white tonight. His brother was wearing his old number—twelve. Keith turned away from him toward the home team bleachers. Bruce looked to see what had captured his brother's attention and picked out Kelly in her band uniform, second row from the top. She made a cute drummer. Her long dark hair and light-colored eyes reminded him of someone he'd thought was pretty cute back in high school.

Now he knew that someone was smokin' hot.

Scanning the crowd to the left of the band, about halfway down, he found his mother. Eva and John were going over the program of players, which Bruce had forgotten to grab.

Farther down on the right, Lucky sat holding Chance while leaning over Cait to talk to the boys on the bench. Bruce didn't see the coach. Or Mitzi. But her father was sitting behind the team, near Bruce's older brother and sister-in-law. He watched as they exchanged a few words.

Cait spotted him and waved. She nudged Lucky and his brother looked up. Lucky, not to be confused with Luke—though they'd often been confused—was Bruce's only full blood brother. He made Chance wave a chubby fist even though the baby, now almost one, couldn't pick his uncle out in the crowd.

Bruce waved back. Yeah, he could count his blessings. Parents who loved him, a younger brother who worshipped him—most of the time. And an older brother he envied.

From his vantage point he could see the JROTC Drill Team forming up outside the double doors, which had been opened wide for the occasion. They wore white ascots, white gloves and black berets with their junior paramilitary uniforms. Wooden rifles painted white with black plated accents added just the right snap to their routine.

Behind them stood the color guard.

And behind that line of flag bearers he caught a glimpse of Mitzi and Estrada in deep discussion. Even though Estrada was an active duty reservist and taught JROTC at the high school, it seemed odd that the coach would be wearing his dress uniform on a game night.

Then Bruce caught a glimpse of the folded jersey in Estrada's hands. Number fifteen. Zahn.

Realization hit Bruce with the full force of a rocket-propelled grenade.

"Can I see that program?" he asked the couple seated next to him. Sure enough, Freddie's number was being retired tonight. And no one had bothered to tell him.

Not Mitzi. Not his family.

When the hell had he become the homeless guy?

KEITH LAUNCHED a three-point shot at the buzzer and Englewood edged out Alameda 86–85 for the win. In the midst of all the excitement, Mitzi stopped trying so hard not to notice him.

Bruce knew, because he'd spent the entire game watching her. He wasn't going to make a scene. This was Freddie's night. He just wanted to know *why* she felt the need to exclude him. Why Estrada had stood at the podium while he sat on the sidelines.

Only one of them had been Freddie's friend and teammate. On the court and in combat where it really counted. And it wasn't the schoolteacher. Of course, only one of them could say he'd let both Freddie and Mitzi down.

Bruce remained seated while the crowd filed out around him. Fred Zahn Sr. caught sight of him and waved on his way out the door, presumably to head off the crowd before they beat him back to the Broadway Bar & Bowl.

"We'll meet you over at the bowling alley," his mom called out as she and John passed by his bleachers. "Lucky said they'd give you a ride."

Lucky and Cait were slower to cross over to his side. They had Chance's baby stuff to haul, and Cait had to be at least eight months pregnant.

"You just going to sit there?" Lucky stood at the foot of the bleachers.

"I'm wondering why nobody bothered to tell me they were retiring number fifteen tonight."

Cait tucked a strand of blond hair behind her ear. "I'm so sorry, Bruce," his beautiful, blue-eyed sister-in-law apologized. That's all he wanted, an apology. Lucky got an "I told you so" as Cait balanced Chance high on her hip to compensate for her baby bump.

His brother wasted no time in clearing the bleachers two steps at a time against the thinning crowd. "I guess we all just assumed Mitzi would say something."

"Yeah, well, she didn't."

Lucky stopped below him with one foot resting on the step above. "At least Keith—"

"He didn't."

Lucky seemed surprised by that. "Well, you made it, that's what's important. Cut us some slack.

We're happy to have you home, but a little advance warning would have been nice. Nobody knew you were flying in on that red-eye this morning. Or that you'd even taken the recruiting assignment. Last I'd heard you were hoping for something closer to San Diego. Communication works both ways, little bro."

Bruce shifted his gaze to center court. Now that the bleachers were cleared, players headed to their respective locker rooms. Coaches paused to shake hands. The visiting and assistant coaches followed their teams, while Estrada went back to the bench where Mitzi waited for him.

"Don't go there," Lucky said, forcing Bruce's attention back to him. "She's moved on."

"I'm aware of that."

"So come spend time with the family. We'll have pizza and beer and maybe even bowl a few frames if the lanes aren't already too crowded. We can listen to Keith brag about tonight's three-pointer at the buzzer and you can shut him up with all your state championship wins."

Lucky had bragging rights of his own. He'd been a point guard in his day.

Bruce shook his head. Any other night he would have. But that half sandwich and half bag of popcorn already felt like lead in his gut.

"Can we at least give you a ride home?"

"I'll walk."

Lucky hesitated.

"I'm fine," Bruce said. "Just tell them I'm tired after a long first day and that early flight."

It wasn't far from the truth and at least got his brother moving in the right direction. Lightening Cait's load by carting the baby and the diaper bag to the exit, Lucky shook his head at something his wife said.

Bruce hated pity more than anything. But coming from a guy who'd traded his motorcycle for a minivan, what an insult.

He knew it wasn't going to be easy seeing her with another man. He just hadn't known it was going to be this hard.

The Englewood High School coach had taken off his uniform jacket sometime during the game and looked like the real deal with his loosened tie and rolled-up sleeves, sweating out the win with his team. Bruce refused to look away as the other man put his arms around Mitzi.

A touch here. A brush there. Enough already.

The couple exchanged a few words and a casual kiss, which put the pink in her cheeks. Estrada sent Bruce a look on his way to the locker room, intended to keep Bruce in line.

Finally the crowd dwindled down to two.

The tap of her heels echoed as she crossed the court. She was wearing her service dress blue uniform tonight—a dark navy blue skirt and suit jacket with gold buttons worn over a white blouse with a black neck tab.

The same uniform she'd worn to Freddie's funeral. After which she'd rushed straight to Bruce's hospital room. He'd been groggy from surgery and that long flight out of Germany.

It was his hand she'd been holding then.

She'd had such a sad smile.

Now look at her. A spring in her step.

And a promotion.

The gold on her left sleeve identified her as a chief petty officer. He knew she carried her white gloves and black-and-white combination cap in her left hand, keeping the right hand free to salute— even though the Navy and Marine Corps did not salute uncovered. And that the overcoat draped over her arm hid two gold stripes, one for every four years of service.

She wore her dark brown hair braided and pinned.

He liked it when she took those braids down. She couldn't wear it that way in uniform, and out of uniform a ponytail was her default hairstyle.

Except in the bedroom.

Knowing that he couldn't have her didn't stop him from wanting her.

She stopped at the foot of his bleachers. "Do you need help getting down?" What made that question worse was the sincerity in her voice.

"I'm not a cat stuck up in a tree. You don't have to call the fire department, Chief."

"Allow me to rephrase my question, Calhoun," she said with equal sarcasm. "Are you coming down? Or am I coming up?"

"Suit yourself."

She tossed her overcoat, her hat and everything else she carried onto the bench at the bottom. Then she removed her pumps to carry them as she climbed the bleachers in her prim and proper uniform skirt. He leaned back on his elbows and stretched out his good leg as she made her way toward him.

The bleachers were steep and she was afraid of heights. "How'd you ever climb aboard a Seahawk?"

"They're on the ground when I get in."

But helicopters weren't designed to stay on the ground. She had to jump out over water to do her job. And at some point she had to get herself and her casualties back into that hovering helo. There was a lot to admire about a woman who wasn't afraid to conquer her fears.

When he wasn't pissed off at her.

CHAPTER FIVE

"WHY DIDN'T YOU TELL ME?" Bruce asked once she'd reached the top. Mitzi sat next to him, so close they were almost touching. He shifted forward uncomfortably.

"I'm sorry." She dangled her black pumps out over knees pressed firmly together.

"We spent the entire day in each other's company. And you never once thought to say, 'Calhoun, you might want to polish up your brass and head over to the high school tonight.'"

"I said I'm sorry." The color Dan had put in her cheeks turned to an angry red.

"I'm wearing sweats—"

"It's not always about you, Calhoun."

"Then what is it about?" He held her clear blue gaze until she was the one who had to look away first. It was about something more complicated than he could put into words. But it wasn't like her not to have a few choice ones for him if she was that mad. "He was my best friend, Mitz—"

"He was *my* brother." Her uniform jacket hummed. She heaved a weary sigh. "I'm glad you found your way here. I should have told you."

"That a cell phone in your pocket? Or are you just happy to see me?"

She frowned as she reached into her pocket and pulled out her BlackBerry. "It's Dan," she said, checking the number.

"By all means." Bruce waved her to answer it. The guy had just headed to the locker room a few minutes ago. Had he even left the building yet?

Checking up on *him,* no doubt.

"Hi," she said into the phone, pausing to listen while Bruce got out his own cell and sent her a text. She glanced at her screen, then sideways at him. "No," she continued, turning her back to him. "I'm tired—it's been a long day. I think I'm just going to head home." She paused to listen. "See you tomorrow, then? Good night, Dan."

"Ouch," Bruce said as she closed her phone. "Lying to the new boyfriend."

"I wasn't lying. He'd promised to take the team out for pizza. I'm tired. And I'm headed home."

He raised an eyebrow, waiting for the *and he's not my boyfriend* part of the denial. It never came.

"You forgot to mention I'm walking you home." He picked up his discarded popcorn bag and stood.

In her stocking feet, shoes in hand, she only came up to his shoulder. "Maybe I drove."

He called her bluff. "Didn't see your car in the lot."

"That doesn't mean you're walking me home, Calhoun."

"I'm headed in that direction."

"You don't even know where I live." She took a step down and reached back as if to help him, but stopped when he continued foot-over-foot right past her.

"You're walking down stairs," she said, amazed.

"The first step is always a leap of faith." He hopped to the ground and held out his hand, glad he still had the power to amaze her. To his surprise she put her hand in his and let him help her down. Her touch was softer somehow, reminding him that being behind a desk all these months meant she wasn't strapped into a rescue harness and dangling from the end of a rope.

Did she resent him for that?

She continued to hold on to him to steady herself as she put her shoes back on.

"I guess you could walk me home." She relented as he helped her with her overcoat. "Since you're headed in that direction anyway."

"Ever do that to me?" he asked on the way to the gym's double doors.

"What?"

"Let a guy walk you home, knowing I wouldn't like it."

She rolled her eyes as they passed the janitor and Bruce tossed his empty popcorn bag into the oversize trash bin.

"Oh, come on." He zipped up his sweat jacket as he shoved against the crossbar. He held the door for her, then let it fall closed behind them. "We had a long-distance relationship for almost ten years. We were apart more often than we were together."

"Six and a half years," she said, adjusting her hat once they were outside. "We haven't been *together* for several months now. And we weren't together my last two years of high school."

"What about what's-his-name?" he asked as they cut across the student parking lot.

"Who are you talking about?"

"Your old crew chief."

"Webb?"

"Ever spend time with him while we were together…?"

"Sleep with him, you mean?" She sighed heavily. "Let it go, Calhoun!"

He didn't want to let it go. He had to know.

"How'd you meet Estrada?" Shoving his hands into his pockets, he stopped under a streetlight and turned to look at her. "Was tonight his idea or yours?"

She kept walking and he had no choice but to move if he wanted to follow her home.

"Mine, I guess." She drew the lapels of her overcoat together and crossed her arms against the frigid air. He resisted the urge to put an arm around her for warmth, knowing his gesture would be rejected. "We met in front of the trophy case in the hall," she continued. "He introduced himself as the new basketball coach. And I pointed out Freddie in a couple old team photos. I guess he suggested it—" she shrugged "—but I was onboard from the start. What difference does it make?"

What difference? He'd bet she didn't point him out in any of those old photos.

"And then the coach just started stopping by in the mornings with coffee. Sounds like a pretty smooth operator to me."

"Takes one to know one."

They continued for a few blocks in silence. "I don't think I like him," he said on a serious note.

"Too bad. I like him and you don't get a say anymore."

"Danny boy is not going to like it when he finds out I walked you home after you blew him off. That's all I'm saying." And if he felt a little smug in saying so, well, he couldn't help it.

"This is where we say good-night, Calhoun." Mitzi stopped in front of a duplex with a *sold* sign out front.

"You bought a house?"

About two blocks away from where they'd both grown up.

It shouldn't surprise him. She'd always been a bit of a homebody, even while deployed. Wasn't that their issue? She wanted to settle down and he didn't?

"Freddie left me some money," she admitted. "I'm renovating it." She didn't have to point out the obvious, with the Dumpster parked out front. "I plan to rent out half. Maybe generate a second income for myself. I don't know." She shrugged.

"Looks like quite a project."

"It is." She nodded. He nodded. "Good night," she repeated.

They'd never shared a house, or an apartment. But he'd always thought that someday…

"Why didn't you tell me?" he asked again.

"I didn't think you'd come," she admitted. "And I didn't want to be disappointed."

Again was implied.

When she was halfway up the front steps he called after her. "Mitzi." He hesitated, choosing his next words carefully. "People grieve in different ways. I'm not using that as an excuse…. I'm just saying I'm sorry I ever disappointed you."

MITZI WAS TOO TIRED to sleep. Her bed was a futon in the middle of what would someday be the living room. She kept a flashlight handy in case she needed to get up in the middle of the night. And an iPod dock/clock radio to make sure she got up in the morning.

The glaring red numbers told her it was 1:23 a.m., just two minutes later than the last time she'd looked. She turned her back on the clock, punched her pillow again, but couldn't stop tossing and turning.

She'd never lied to him. Not the way he'd misled her.

Reaching for the clock to turn those obtrusive numbers around, she knocked her cell phone from the futon to the floor. Picking it up reminded her of Bruce's text message. Not knowing what to expect, she pressed the Okay button to view it.

Still here.

No kidding. It was bad enough he'd occupied her every waking moment today. Did he have to climb into bed with her, as well?

Not literally, of course.

Even if he was the only man she'd ever been with, she didn't know who that man was anymore.

People grieve in different ways....

And some not at all.

At 1:25 a.m. she gave up ever falling asleep and

got out of bed. She padded across the floor in her bare feet and pajamas.

She'd acquired few possessions in her adult life. It wasn't that long ago she'd driven from California home to Colorado with everything she owned packed into her Honda CR-V. Between moving back home and buying her own place, she still felt like a woman in transition. Admittedly she should have unpacked boxes by now, but she hadn't. So Mitzi knew exactly which file box to grab, along with her cell phone and the comforter off her bed, when she went out to the front porch, which at least had overhead lighting.

Wrapped in her warm blanket, she sat on the stoop and opened the box containing her brother's personal effects.

A cell phone with no service.

Before it had been disconnected she'd listened to the recorded message for his voice mail over and over again. "Hi, you've reached Freddie. Can't come to the phone right now. Leave a message."

She used to call his phone long after he was gone, saying all those things she wished she'd said while he was still alive. The day his phone service was cut had been one of her worst days, because she hadn't thought to save his recording.

She'd been smarter about uploading his photos and phone book. Tonight she erased them from the phone's memory. Then she slipped the phone into the padded envelope she'd prepared with prepaid postage to Cell Phones for Soldiers, the brainchild of a young brother and sister.

Brother and sister. Freddie would have teased her for that sentimentality. But it was time to let go of his cell phone and let it do someone else some good. For security purposes the donated phones weren't sent overseas. They were sold for cash, which was used to purchase prepaid calling cards.

With Thanksgiving and Christmas coming she couldn't think of a better gift to give someone. She set the envelope aside to mail tomorrow and reached into the box again. This time she pulled out an open pack of gum and helped herself to a piece.

Only after she put the gum in her mouth and realized it was a little hard to chew did she think to check the expiration date on the package. Sure enough.

Expired last year.

Funny how it seemed like only yesterday she'd met Freddie and Bruce in Kuwait. There were days when she had to remind herself that she couldn't just pick up the phone and call her brother. Or Calhoun for that matter. It had been more than a year now of missing them both.

Spitting the gum back into the wrapper, she set

it aside to throw away later. She left the open pack and all the unopened packs in the box.

Freddie had gum with him at all times. She'd forever associate the smell of cinnamon with him.

Digging through the box, she found pocket change, a comb, his diving watch and everything from legal papers to some of the letters she'd written him from boot camp. She still had to weed through it all—just not tonight.

Tonight she'd opened this box for another reason.

It came in a small black velvet box, which she'd tucked away with Freddie's belongings. But she'd known there would come a day when she'd have to deal with it.

She pried open the lid to her engagement ring. White gold. Beautiful in its simplicity.

A one-carat—more than he could afford—pear-cut diamond. Looked like a teardrop to Mitzi.

Fifteen months earlier
Balboa Naval Medical Center
San Diego, California

MITZI PULLED UP to the loading zone in her new Honda CR-V, then scrambled around to the passenger side to open the door. A young hospital corpsman wheeled Bruce to the curb and laid his crutches and overnight bag across the backseat.

Bruce's doctor had given him a weekend pass in advance of his hospital discharge next month so they could spend some time together before Mitzi had to report to Pensacola, Florida, for five weeks of Navy recruiter school.

Despite a forecast that called for rain, Mitzi wore a bright floral-print sundress for the occasion. Bruce was wearing a baggy gray T-shirt and sweats with the empty pant leg folded and pinned out of the way. The loose-fitting sweats emphasized the amount of weight he'd lost recently.

He refused help getting out of the wheelchair or into the car. Grabbing the open door, he hopped up on his good leg. Then hopped in an awkward half circle until he could push that tight tush of his up into the seat.

Before she could close the door he had it closed. Mitzi thanked the corpsman for his help and circled back to the driver's side. "Seat belt," she reminded Bruce while securing her own.

He started to fasten his seat belt, then stopped to pull a copy of *Bride* magazine out from under his butt.

"Sorry." Mitzi took the bridal magazine from him and tucked it between their seats. The backseat was full of magazines with white gowns on the covers. Until she'd started Navy counselor school four weeks ago, in preparation for Navy recruiter school—and to extend her stay in San Diego—she'd spent a lot of time in waiting rooms.

Bruce clicked his seat belt into place as she pulled away from the curb. Her car still had that new-car smell and he commented on it. "I would have gone car shopping with you."

If you'd *waited* was implied.

"My dad was here," she said, feeling the need to defend her decision. "And I wanted to take advantage of the cash-for-clunkers program."

Going new-car shopping with her father while he was here seemed like the least she could do. After Freddie's funeral he'd pressed her to spend the rest of her leave at home, but she wanted to stay near Bruce.

"I thought we'd picnic at the lighthouse," she said, determined to remain upbeat. After two surgeries, the first to try to save his knee and the second to take it, Bruce had every right to be cranky.

Nothing seemed to stop his pain.

But at this point she had to wonder how much of it was in his head. Real or imagined, she didn't know how to help him. Not when he pushed her away.

His doctors here were optimistic about his future mobility. And while Bruce had started out just as optimistic, something inside him had changed after that second surgery. He seemed to be experiencing more pain than before. And more phantom limb symptoms.

"May as well head straight to the motel," he said, checking the sky. "It's going to rain."

"Since when has a little rain ever dampened one of our picnics?" Rain used to be their favorite weather for lovemaking. She continued driving toward the park.

There'd been plenty of day trips and overnight passes over these three months. But they'd put off sex for so long now she felt apprehensive about this weekend.

The closer they came to the lighthouse the quieter he grew. It was probably his least favorite place on earth. And the one place she needed to be right now. Cabrillo National Monument overlooked Fort Rosecrans Military Reservation. Navy SEALs requested burial here because of its view of the bay and Naval Special Warfare Command.

Mitzi saw the pain etched into Bruce's face as he popped the lid to his painkillers, and she wished she'd driven straight to the motel.

"Do you need some water?" She offered him her bottle.

He shook his head and swallowed dry more pills than the prescribed dose, she suspected.

"What about a Pez dispenser?" she muttered under her breath.

He gave her a dirty look before leaning back against the headrest and closing his eyes.

She already knew how this weekend was going to end. He'd insist she stop by a liquor store on the way to the motel, where he'd drink a fifth of something until he passed out. She'd alternate between staring at the walls and pacing the floor—so helpless and out of her mind with worry that she couldn't wait to get him back to the hospital.

She'd hoped, this being their last weekend together for a while, things would be different.

The first spattering of rain fell as she entered the park. Mitzi flicked on the headlights and windshield wipers and drove through the military reservation. "I guess we'll have to skip the picnic after all."

He muttered something that sounded a lot like "I told you so," and she had to bite her tongue.

"I need to make a quick stop first." Pulling off to the side of the road, she opened the glove compartment and dug out the park map so she could find her brother's numbered plot. "The headstones are supposed to be up in his section now."

"Let's just go. You're not going to be able to see anything anyway." He was right, of course. The rain was coming down harder now. The uneven beat against the car turned into a steady drum, broken only by the swish of the wipers.

The windows started to fog and she turned on

the defroster. Leaning across him to peer out his window, she pointed to a white marble headstone in a sea of white marble headstones. "That's it there, I think. And right next to him is Luke—"

She turned to find Bruce staring at her. Medication had softened the tense lines of his face. He almost looked like himself. She really didn't begrudge him the relief of pain pills, and she traced the lines that lingered. First with her fingertips, and then with kisses.

He kissed her back, softly.

She couldn't remember the last time he hadn't fallen into a drug-induced sleep during foreplay. If he managed to stay awake long enough for her to even get him aroused, he'd simply excuse himself and go to the bathroom.

As if she didn't know what was going on in there.

Careful of his stump, she moved across his lap. Though he rarely allowed her a glimpse of it, she could feel his tightly wrapped stump through his sweatpants. She'd never seen it without the white surgical bandage or the beige compression bandage he'd graduated to once his stump had healed. Though she knew he had to wrap it daily, sometimes several times a day.

Once she straddled him completely, her open thighs communicating her need, she felt him tense.

He turned his head to break the kiss.

"Sorry, did I hurt you?"

"A cemetery? Is this how you get your kicks these days?"

That was just plain mean. "An airplane hangar ring any bells?" Given a minute, she could have come up with a dozen *inappropriate* places they'd had sex.

"Mitz," he insisted, "please, get off me. We need to talk."

Nothing good ever started with *Please, get off me*. She sank back in her seat. "Okay."

"I'm not going home with you."

She had orders to their hometown recruiting station in Englewood. Following recruiter school she'd be headed there. Meanwhile, he was supposed to put in for a medical discharge. And once his hospital stay was up he'd be free to return home with her.

Where they'd have some semblance of normalcy until her enlistment was up. They'd get married. Buy a house.

Have the kind of life she'd dreamed of having with him, but never thought possible. "We talked about—"

"Recovery for an above-the-knee amputee takes twelve to fifteen months of intensive therapy. I've got the best chance of rehabilitation if I stay here."

"You know I want whatever's best for you."

"It's not that," he said, looking at her with an intensity she found hard to read. "A record number of amputees are returning to duty."

He meant to combat. She stared past him out the window at her brother's grave. "How long have you felt this way?" She knew how he felt about being a Marine. She'd just thought that once he was discharged things would be different.

"For a while," he admitted.

"Why wait until now to tell me?"

She saw the answer in his eyes—because he wanted her to accept recruiting duty. Wanted to send her home without him.

"I think we should postpone the wedding," he said, ignoring her question. "For…a while."

"Postpone? We're in a permanent holding pattern already."

"If you don't want to wait for me, *fine*."

Fine? She sucked in her breath. "I've waited my whole life for you, Calhoun. The white dress… The walk down the aisle… All I dream about is dancing with you at our wedding."

"I *will* walk again."

She choked back a laugh. "It feels like you're walking now. Away from me."

His jaw tightened. He looked out his window. "You knew what you were getting into when I proposed."

Did she? She'd fallen in love with a charming boy who was a competitive basketball player. She loved the man who was courageous and committed. But where did his dedication to the Corps end and his devotion to her begin?

Everything had changed when Freddie was killed.

"I need a break from all of this." He swept his hand to encompass everything from her brother's grave to the bridal magazine. He should have just pointed at her.

"Yeah," she agreed with a heavy dose of sarcasm. "I need one, too."

"Just take me back to the hospital," he said, digging out his pill bottle.

If it hadn't been raining, her ring finger wouldn't have been swollen, and she could have twisted it off and thrown it at him. Instead Mitzi had to keep it together while she turned the car around and drove back to Balboa.

By the time she'd parked the car and gone to the passenger side to help him, he had his crutches and was out the door.

She grabbed some magazines to help keep her dry and his overnight bag. Did he expect her to follow with it? Or keep it? She stood in the rain watching him go. Planting his crutches, swinging his weight forward, planting his single foot. His sweats were getting wet from the rain.

This wasn't how their relationship was supposed to end.

She missed whatever elevator he'd taken to his ward. Barely slowing for the "Caution: wet floor" signs, she reached his room right behind him. Half the beds were empty because it was the weekend. A couple other guys she'd come to know over the past three months were playing cards and one was napping.

He was halfway to his bed when his crutch skidded in a puddle of his own making. "Let me help—"

"Will you leave me alone!" he yelled, loud enough to make his roommates look up. He twisted around and she dropped the wet magazines trying to get out of his way. "What don't you get?"

"Any of it, I guess." Wiping away her running mascara, she stood in the middle of the room. Wet hair. Wet dress. "I get that you're hurting right now, Calhoun. But I'm hurting, too, and you don't get to take it out on me." She wasn't even trying to hide her tears. And he didn't look away. "You don't have anything to prove, not to me."

She dumped his overnight bag on top of the scattered magazines. Prescription pill bottles and those little liquor bottles he tried to hide went rolling across the floor. "But you'd better clean yourself up and get your act together. Then get your ass home, Marine. Because I am not *waiting* for you forever."

She left his hospital room in tears.

CHAPTER SIX

BRUCE WALKED INTO WORK the following morning—with two Egg McMuffins and two cups of McDonald's coffee—to find a black box on his desk. He set down the tray and picked it up.

"He'd want you to have it," Mitzi said, sneaking up on him from the alcove. Like him, she was wearing her combat utilities today.

Bruce lifted the lid. "Thank you," he said past the lump in his throat.

"He loved you like a brother." She crossed the room to take his left hand in hers. Turning his wrist, she unbuckled his dive watch and replaced it with her brother's.

"Ditto." There was something so intimate about the act of her changing out his watch that he simply surrendered to it.

"Don't make this any harder than it is, okay?"

"Okay." Distracted by her bent head and the whiff of whatever the fragrance was in her hair, he never even saw it coming.

She placed a small black velvet box in the palm of his upturned hand. "I should have given this back to you sooner. I'm sorry."

Sorry it was over?

Or sorry she hadn't given it back to him sooner?

AFTER THAT QUICK BITE at his desk—and he didn't mean the Egg McMuffins he'd thrown away—they'd gone their separate ways for most of the morning.

Bruce had stopped by the high school to meet with the principal and secure his invitation to Career Day. He might not want to be here, and Mitzi definitely didn't want him here, but he still had a job to do.

Englewood High School was a public school, and as long as he didn't do anything to piss off the principal or the school board, no one could bar him from recruiting there. Least of all his kid brother.

For a late lunch Bruce found himself headed down the street toward the Broadway Bar & Bowl. There were no bowlers, so the lanes were dark.

Behind the counter a gum-popping matron with big hair and horn-rimmed glasses—a throwback to the place's fifties theme—sprayed down rental shoes with Lysol.

A few regulars sat at the bar inside an even dimmer lounge, where the smell of stale beer and nuts refused to be overpowered by the smell of disinfectant. Big screens mounted in every corner played highlights from a recent Nuggets game.

Peanut shells crunched beneath Bruce's boots as he took a seat at the bar. "Diet Coke and a cheeseburger."

The bartender—and also owner—of the Broadway Bar & Bowl whirled around with a wide grin on his face. "Well, look what the wind blew in! I was thinking I might see you sometime today, Calhoun. My daughter with you?" The senior—and now only—Fred Zahn checked behind Bruce for Mitzi.

"Just me."

Fred reached across the bar and slapped Bruce on the shoulder several times for good measure. "Let me get you something stronger than a soft drink."

"A little early in the day for me," Bruce admitted, sheepishly.

"Diet Coke it is, then," Fred said, drawing the soda from the tap. He added a cherry, like when Bruce was a kid, then set the glass on a coaster in front of him. "Two blue plate specials," he shouted to the cook in back. "How the hell are you, son?"

"Good. Better," he amended, taking a sip of his drink. The last time Bruce had seen Fred Zahn was after Freddie's funeral while Bruce was still in the hospital.

Fred nodded in understanding. "Thought I'd run into you here after the game. Saw you across the way."

"Yeah, got there late. Wound up in the visitor bleachers." Bruce played with the cherry in his drink, not wanting to go into detail about the rest of his evening.

"Ahh. Watching your brother last night—" he shook his head "—brought back a lot of memories."

Bruce could look in any direction and see pictures on the wall of Freddie and him with a basketball.

For twenty years the Zahn family had lived next door to the Calhouns. There was a lot of history there that made it impossible for him to just walk away from Mitzi, even if he wanted to. And especially when he didn't.

Behind the bar, portraits of Freddie and Mitzi in their respective dress uniforms hung side by side. A black ribbon draped the corner of Freddie's picture.

Bruce found himself looking up at the latest addition.

Fred glanced over his shoulder. "Mitzi's doing. Said we needed some kind of memorial. Last night, too."

Bruce touched the watch on his wrist, glad she still thought enough of him to give him a memento of her brother. Especially since it was really over between them.

"They should've retired your number along with his," Fred said, following Bruce's silence.

"Nah." Bruce shook his head. He'd rather see his old number in action. Let his brother get some mileage out of it. Freddie would have felt the same way. If he'd had a brother. The day they'd enlisted they'd hung their state championship jerseys in back by the pool tables and had their own unofficial number-retiring ceremony.

"Come bowl a few frames with me," Fred invited, throwing back the bar gate. "They'll bring us our food."

"I haven't bowled in a while," Bruce hedged.

A while meaning post amputation.

"It's like riding a bicycle."

"Forgetting how is not what I'm worried about."

"I was thinking more like hard as hell at first. But you'll get the hang of it after a few bumps and bruises."

He'd gotten the hang of a stationary bicycle through trial and error, and now he worked out on one religiously. Mountain biking was on his to-do list come spring. He was not going to let being a LAK hold him back.

Why not bowling? Why not now?

The alley was empty.

Fred grabbed his bowling bag from an unlocked locker. Mitzi's dad was fit and trim and still looked like the cop he'd once been. "Audrey," he called out, "lane seven. Size thirteens," he said, recalling Bruce's exact shoe size. "Make that a new box of right-handed bowling shoes. Let's try a left-handed pair, too."

Bruce went looking for a ball with just the right fit and feel to it. Eventually he settled on a neon-green one.

"The kids like the bright colors," Fred apologized. "And don't get me started on the light shows."

"I don't mind," Bruce said, carrying the bright ball over to lane seven.

"Kids used to stop by for French fries and a game or two after school. Now they hurry home to video bowl on their Wii systems. I had to take out two pool tables to update the game room with oversize driving and dancing games just to get them in the door. And don't get me started on the competition out there with those fast food chains popping up all over the place. Did you see the new Smashburger on the corner?"

"You want the pair of rentals, too?" Audrey handed over a stack of shoe boxes with the rentals on top.

"May as well," Fred said.

Bruce was already unlacing his boots.

"Rentals are universal," Fred explained. "Sliders on both shoes. But we keep plenty of new shoes and balls in stock this time of year."

Bruce seemed to recall that information filed in the back of his brain somewhere. He'd hung out here with Freddie and Mitzi a lot as a kid.

"Right-handed bowling shoes have a gripper on the right and a slider on the left. You're right-handed, but we could try the left-handed shoes. See how that works with your leg."

By the end of their first game Bruce had tried every combination of gripper and slider. He was back to the right-handed bowling shoes. "Didn't even break a hundred," Bruce said, standing at the ball return with his hand over the blower and looking up at his electronic score. His cheeseburger, sitting on the back table, was all but forgotten as he picked up the ball again.

"Never mind the score."

"It's not the score so much as the gutter balls."

He didn't trust his artificial leg in the slide.

"I could put in the bumpers," Fred said.

Bruce hoped the man was joking.

"Thanks, but no thanks."

Fred looked him over with a critical eye. "What's a leg going for these days?"

Bruce could pretend he'd misunderstood. Most

people were interested in the cost of his prosthesis. But that's not what Fred was asking. "Thirty-five grand."

That's how much he'd been paid by Uncle Sam for the loss of his leg. Roughly the cost of a good prosthesis. But he'd been given one of those—more than one of those—too.

"Invest that money in your future and you won't go wrong," Fred advised.

Bruce hadn't touched a dime. There were a lot of mixed emotions attached to that money.

Mitzi had purchased something tangible with the money Freddie had left her—a house. A home.

She'd been right about him—he wasn't ready for that. Not if settling down meant standing still.

He hadn't realized just how ready she was until she'd accused him of walking away from her before he could even walk.

"Your new leg a C-Leg?" Fred continued.

A C-Leg was a computerized leg. Microprocessors sensed and corrected movement for a natural gait. "With modifications, yes."

Just call me the hundred-thousand-dollar man.

A good leg prosthesis ran around thirty, thirty-five grand. But thanks to the Special Warfare Association he had the best custom leg money could buy, a heavy-duty, high-tech knee capable of artificial intelligence.

High-speed pattern recognition responded to changes in speed, load and terrain. He could walk, he could run, he could jump, he could climb and he could swim—all without changing his leg.

What he couldn't do *yet* was bowl.

"Try a five-step approach," Fred suggested.

Because of his height, Bruce had always used a four-step. Five steps would mean shortening his stride and starting off on his artificial foot.

Leading with his left felt awkward at first, but after several trips to the foul line he felt comfortable enough to swing his arm and let go of the ball. Before he knew it he, and his computerized knee, had the mechanics down and a measure of his old confidence back.

By the time school let out Bruce was bowling with a respectable spin on his ball and had broken that elusive hundred. Still a long way from his 260 average.

"See what I mean." Fred commented on the lack of an afternoon crowd. "If I thought Mitzi could make a living at it, I'd leave the business to her and retire."

"You think Mitzi would want the bowling alley?" Bruce asked, trying not to sound too interested. He shouldn't care what Mitzi wanted. Whatever it was, it wasn't him. But her enlistment was up soon and he was curious about her plans.

"Hell, I don't know," Fred said. "But I'm ready

to retire. This summer marks my thirtieth police academy reunion. Of the six guys still on active duty, four of them are retiring from the Englewood Police Department this year. You might want to think about applying. I'd put in a good word for you."

"Appreciate it, Fred, but I'm going to stick with the military." They could sit him behind a desk for now, but he was capable of more, and once he proved it he'd be back in action. "Besides," he said, trying to keep his tone light, "I don't think the Englewood P.D. is looking for a one-legged bowler with a sixty-nine handicap to round out their league."

Bruce was just guessing at his handicap. But he'd bet he was pretty close.

"Maybe not," Fred agreed. "But a decorated Marine…they might overlook your handicap."

Of course, neither of them was talking about bowling.

A FEW FRAMES LATER Bruce's newfound confidence turned into overconfidence. Mitzi strolled in with Estrada and a couple of his Army recruiter buddies. Feeling as if everyone's eyes were on him, Bruce counted out his steps. Nothing less than a strike would do at this moment.

So he went for it.

Deep into the controlled slide his left foot

slipped. He released the ball into the gutter and stopped himself from falling by shifting his weight to his right foot and catching himself with his right hand.

"Are you all right?" Mitzi called.

"I'm fine," he said as he picked himself up from his awkward crouch.

"You sure?"

"I said I was," he snapped. Too late he saw the hurt in her eyes. Before she shut him out.

"Help me get these boys their usual beers," her father said.

BY THE TIME HAPPY HOUR rolled around the Broadway Bar & Bowl had a respectable crowd for a weeknight. Bruce sat at a table with Mitzi, Estrada, Army recruiters Mike and Ike—whose real name, or at least last name, was Ikelhoff—and Annie, an Air Force recruiter who posted the highest numbers of any recruiter in the district for good reason—the blonde was easy on the eyes and a real go-getter.

For his part, Bruce hung out in observation mode. The lack of an after-school crowd might have more to do with the steady stream of teachers and off-duty cops, he thought.

Still, there were enough twentysomethings from the music venue next door at the Gothic Theatre for him to watch his fellow recruiters in action.

"Let me get these out of your way," Audrey

said, setting down their drinks and loading up with empties.

"Thanks." Bruce tossed enough bills to her tray to cover their tab. He'd switched from Diet Coke to club soda at the bar as the night progressed. It wasn't anyone's business what he was or wasn't drinking. Club soda just made it easier for him to fit in with the crowd.

"Hate to do this to you, Dan," Mike was saying, "but the girlfriend insisted we spend Thanksgiving back east with her folks. Maybe Ike here—" he nudged Ike "—or Bruce could help chaperone the ski trip."

"Don't worry about it," Estrada said.

Bruce seemed to recall Keith being excited about some ski trip to Vail with the coach. Only seniors were invited and it was a big deal. Coed.

Judging by the way Estrada avoided looking at him, the other man didn't want him to tag along. There could be only one reason for that. Bruce followed Estrada's telltale gaze toward Mitzi.

Coed ski trip? Any male teacher with half a brain would make sure he had at least one female chaperone.

"Yeah, I'll do it," Bruce volunteered.

"Really, it's not necessary," Estrada said. "I'll find someone—"

"You already found someone," Bruce countered.

"Can you ski?" Estrada asked, and the table went quiet.

"With a prosthesis, you mean?" Bruce said. Estrada wouldn't even be asking about his abilities if Bruce hadn't almost fallen right on his ass in front of him. That or Mitzi had mentioned something to him. It bothered him to think Mitzi still saw him as a helpless cripple. "Won't know until I try," he said. "But I was pretty good once."

There was always the option of one-legged skiing.

Estrada nodded in acceptance. Or as Bruce liked to think of it, *defeat.*

"Come on, let's dance," Annie said, dragging Mitzi away from the table and toward the dance-off platform of the "Dance Dance Revolution" arcade game.

Estrada was quick to follow. Ike and Mike grabbed their beers. "You gotta see this," Mike said, encouraging Bruce to tag along.

So Bruce followed the crowd into the arcade. The women stripped down to their T-shirts and camouflage pants, then took up positions on the dance platform.

Mitzi rolled her shoulders as if she meant business, while Annie ignored the beginner settings and chose something more challenging.

Apparently they'd done this before.

Leaning against the back wall near the fire door, Bruce settled in for the show. — —

CHAPTER SEVEN

FROM THE FIRST BEAT of Lady Gaga's "Just Dance" to the last, Mitzi was on her game. She and Annie had every pop, lock and drop of this song down. The screen flashed Perfect after Perfect as they matched their footwork to the lighted floor pad.

The trick wasn't just to hit your mark.

But to make it look as if you were dancing.

Using the platform rail for support, "the cammie twins," as they were known around the bowling alley, made every wave of their "DDR" dance look sexy. A couple of Twister-like moves as they fell back on their hands and popped back to their feet, and the gathering crowd went wild. The machine accelerated through song after song until a single misstep ended their streak.

Mitzi was dripping sweat coming off the platform. She caught Bruce's eye and smiled. He raised his glass in a salute and her smile became strained. Gin or vodka?

She thought he'd given up drinking.

Dan said something and Mitzi turned her attention to him. "What was that?"

"How 'bout it? Think you could come down to my level long enough to show me how to do this?"

"Sure." Mitzi picked a Black Eyed Peas song from the playlist and chose the "suck" setting.

Dan groaned. "I'm not that bad a dancer."

"We'll see," she teased. She took her gaming very seriously. "Let's Get It Started" began. He was right. He wasn't that bad. But it took him a while to get the hang of it. He racked up a lot of misses as they laughed their way through the song.

By the time their turn ended Bruce had slipped out the back door. She hadn't even seen him leave.

Mitzi used *helping my father* as an excuse to stay long after her friends had left the bowling alley. She picked up a discarded drink from the runner along the back wall where Bruce had been standing, and sniffed.

All she could smell was the lemon zest.

She put the glass to her lips for a taste.

"Club soda," her father said, catching her in the act.

"Umm." Her taste buds agreed. Flat club soda. With lemon. She put the glass on the tray with the rest of the glasses she'd helped clear.

"A drunken binge after losing your leg and your

girl doesn't make a man an alcoholic, honey. As a cop, I've seen plenty of problem drinkers, not to mention working in a bar. Liquor's not that boy's problem."

She set the tray down. "Do you think I am?"

"How could you be anyone's problem?" He gave her a squeeze, then swept her into a hug. "That boy loves you."

"Love was never our problem, Dad. And please don't go there. I know you like Bruce."

"I like the other fella, too."

"I'm glad." She gave her dad a nudge but didn't move from his arms. "Because we're both going to be seeing a lot more of him."

Clearly Bruce had chosen the Corps over her, returning home only after he'd been ordered to. She couldn't allow that to mean a step back for her. Which is why she'd had to return his ring today.

"Bruce led me to believe we'd be together if I took this assignment."

"I wanted you back home as much as anyone. And I don't see you blaming me."

"That's different," she said. "I did everything I could so that Bruce and I could be together. And he did everything he could to keep us apart. He chose the Corps over me."

"Did you ever ask him why?"

"I don't know why he seems so hell-bent on returning to the fight. Haven't we all lost enough already? He never even shed a tear for Freddie. Like that makes him a tough guy or something."

Her dad held her even tighter. "Honey, that only means he never let *you* see him cry."

TAKING HIS USUAL ROUTE home from the gym, Bruce cut through the alley. Tonight he'd worked out in shorts because of the unseasonably warm—or rather changeable—Colorado weather.

He'd left the bowling alley shortly after Estrada stepped onto the dance platform. Bruce's C-Leg had limitations, and jumping around to Lady Gaga and The Black Eyed Peas was one of them.

A dog barked at him as he passed a backyard fence. Up ahead a trash can thundered to the ground, then rolled toward the drainage ditch. He heard the trio before he saw them. They were loud enough. Boys in their late teens, early twenties, looking for trouble.

"Where you hiding it, old man?" the first young thug demanded, sitting in the old man's wheelchair while Henry lay sprawled on the ground.

A second young guy, digging through Henry's pack, tossed the old wheelie's leg and other belongings to the ground. "Found it," he said, pulling out a prescription bottle and shaking it. "Sounds freakin' empty."

"Come on, leave him alone," a third boy said,

standing apart from the other two as if he wanted to bolt but didn't have the guts to make up his mind.

"There's gotta be more than that," Thug One said from his wheeled throne with a glance over his shoulder. "Amps always get the good stuff. Now tell me where it is, old man."

Henry spat on the kid's shoes. Thug One lifted himself from the wheelchair just far enough to kick Henry in the face.

"Hey!" Bruce shouted from his end of the alley. He'd been hoping to move in closer before making his presence known.

The boys were startled into looking up. Thug One was the first to recover. He got out of Henry's chair to strut over to Bruce. "What do we have here? Looks like another amp to me."

"Just give him back his meds and go," Bruce said.

"How'd you lose your leg?" The second little shit moved in closer. The big shit tried to circle around to Bruce's flank. But he was the one Bruce was keeping his eye on even though his follower held the bottle. The third stayed where he was.

"Iraq."

"A wreck?" Thug One taunted.

"That's right," Bruce said, refusing to fan the flame. "A wreck."

Thug One flipped out a switchblade. "What do

you say I finish the job and cut you into pieces, amp?"

"Just when I thought we weren't going to have any fun." Controlling the adrenaline rushing through his veins, Bruce very slowly and deliberately set down his gym bag as he gauged the distance to each of the three.

Only one had a knife. The effective range of a knife was punching distance. And he was too stupid to realize Bruce had a longer reach and was trained to punch back. Before he was up out of his crouch the kid made his move.

Jumping back from the straight thrust, Bruce used an X block and a well-timed kick. The instant their forearms connected, Bruce had twisted his attacker's wrist.

The knife hit the ground with a clang.

The shit followed, kissing concrete. "You broke my freakin' arm, amp!" He screamed like a little girl as Bruce pinned him with his good knee and held him in an arm bar.

"Guess you didn't see *Con Air*. Otherwise you'd know better than to mess with a Marine in a back alley, kid. You're not going to get out of this, so quit struggling."

"The Marine in that movie went to prison," Henry pointed out, climbing back into his wheelchair.

"I haven't killed him—*yet*." Bruce put pressure

on the tough guy's arm for emphasis. "Cell phone's in my bag," he said to Henry. "Call 911." A quick look around told him the other tough had fled the scene with the drugs. The last not-so-tough guy hesitated. "Go on, get the hell out of here," Bruce ordered. "Your friend's in enough trouble for the three of you."

Since they were within shouting distance of Englewood's police department, they didn't have long to wait before they heard the screech of sirens. A few minutes later the first black-and-white pulled up with lights flashing.

"He tried to kill me," his attacker accused as he was being hauled off in handcuffs.

Bruce gave the police his statement and a vague description of the other two. "Late teens, early twenties. Hispanic. Dark hair. Dark eyes. Dark clothes. They took his prescription meds. Narcotics," Bruce repeated for the DEA agent called to the scene.

"About a month's supply of OxyContin," Henry added.

Henry refused to let the ambulance take him to the hospital to be checked out. But he accepted an officer's ride to a local shelter for the night. Which meant the old goat was a lot more rattled than he seemed.

The *old goat* was too old to be living on the streets.

After all the excitement died down, Bruce picked up his gym bag and headed home. He didn't know what made him turn two blocks early, but the darkened duplex made him wish he hadn't.

Mitzi's car wasn't in the drive.

Bruce illuminated his wristwatch—a quarter after eleven. He realized it was Freddie's watch and swallowed the lump in his throat for about the hundredth time that day.

"Damn it," he said to no one in particular and kept on walking. What he really wanted was to sit his ass down on her front stoop and wait. And if Mitzi didn't come home?

He didn't have the balls to find out.

MITZI STIFLED A YAWN, which earned her another frown.

"Late night?" Calhoun asked from across the demilitarized zone, with just enough sarcasm to be annoying. He was in a foul mood this Friday morning. Ever since she'd strolled in late with a cup of coffee in her hand.

"What happened to you last night?" she asked, turning it around on him. "One minute you were there and the next you were gone."

"Early to bed, early to rise…and all that jazz."

"Since when?"

"Since the new me," he said. "Besides, I don't think you missed me all that much."

Was he jealous?

"You might want to clue the new boyfriend in on your curfew. Isn't it midnight? What do they call that in the Navy, *Cinderella Liberty?*"

"I'm not a sailor on shore leave. And if you're referring to Dan, he left shortly after you did."

"You don't owe me an explanation, Chief."

"Then quit acting like you need one," she said, prying open her coffee lid as he walked over with the pot to top her off. "If you really want to know why I was up all night…" She paused while he filled. "Thank you." She smashed the lid back on. "Ask the guy in our neighborhood shooting hoops all night. Very annoying. I'm surprised no one called the cops."

After helping her father close up, she hadn't gotten home until after two in the morning. From two blocks away she could hear the lonely echo of a basketball pounding concrete and slamming against the backboard over and over again.

"You know, if you're having trouble sleeping—"

"Don't even say it." He set the coffeepot back on the burner.

"PTSD." She spelled it out. Post-traumatic stress disorder. After all he'd been through? She wouldn't be surprised. "It's nothing to be ashamed—"

"I've had enough counseling," he said tersely.

"Okay."

She was one to talk. She hadn't slept since his

return and it had nothing to do with the trauma of losing her brother. Being near her father all these months, though, had helped.

Would it be such a terrible thing if she decided to stay in Colorado? Get out of the Navy even? She liked hanging out at the bowling alley. And loved helping her father.

She'd been leaning more toward reenlistment. She had eight years in the Navy. Another hitch would put her at twelve. Then she'd be on the downhill side of a twenty-year retirement.

Right now recruiting gave her the best of both worlds—being home while being in the Navy. Not that she didn't miss her old life as a rescue swimmer. She could reenlist and request a reassignment back to Search and Rescue.

It wasn't something she had to decide right this minute. As long as she kept up her recruiting numbers.

"Morning." Mitzi greeted the mail carrier with a smile as he stepped in and handed the mail to Bruce, who was closer to the door. Friday's mail was one of the perks of recruiting.

Bruce stood over her desk sorting it by branch of service. Mitzi tore into the express envelope from the recruiting district first.

She fanned the hockey, basketball and movie tickets the district provided for recruiting purposes. Being visible in the community while in uniform was an important part of the job. "Want to divvy them up?"

Bruce took them in exchange for another envelope from the downtown office addressed to her personally.

She opened it with less enthusiasm. As she read the letter a frown creased her brow.

"Something wrong?" he asked.

"Nothing." She shook her head. "They bumped my October-through-December recruit quota. And they're just now getting around to telling me. Last quarter it was more Navy SEALs they wanted. This time around it's hospital corpsmen."

She folded the letter and put it back into the envelope. Sometimes even the best-laid plans were put to the test. She'd just have to work a little harder if she wanted to keep her current job.

"This ought to cheer you up." He handed her the stack of tickets all rubber banded together, then sat on the corner of her desk to extend two more. When she reached for them, he pulled back. "What'll you give me for them?"

So that was his game. She rolled her eyes. "Nothing."

"*The Nutcracker* ballet." He teased her with them. "Two tickets. Opening night."

How had she missed those?

She held out her hand. "Give them over."

Her father had taken her to see *The Nutcracker*

every year when she was little. The tradition had fallen by the wayside once she'd joined the Navy and never knew where she'd be spending her holiday.

"I want your *hot sheets*."

"No way! You're not getting your hands on my prospects."

"Then you're not getting these tickets." He tucked them inside his breast pocket and pushed to his feet. "I'm starting out at a disadvantage here, Chief. I need all the leverage I can get."

She struggled with it for a moment, then finally said, "One page."

WHEN BRUCE GOT HOME that evening the empty garbage cans were still in front of the house at the end of the drive. He hauled them up to the garage just as Keith stepped out the back door.

"You couldn't put these garbage cans away after school?"

"I was busy," Keith said, texting as he headed toward his silver '90 Thunderbird parked on the street.

"Busy, my ass." Bruce punched in the garage code and waited for the door to rise high enough so he could duck under.

He picked up a basketball on his way out. Shooting hoops was his natural stress reliever. He'd just have to be a little more conscientious about not keeping the neighbors up at night. Headlights from a car pulling in next door illuminated him as he punched in the code again to close the garage door.

The headlights dimmed and Mitzi got out of her CR-V.

"Hi," she said, continuing around to the back of her vehicle.

"Laundry?" Bruce asked as he stepped in to help unload.

"Moving back home temporarily. I have contractors and painters coming starting next week." She glanced down at his leg as she handed him a basket of clothes.

He wore workout shorts, and this would be the first time she'd seen his C-Leg. He was too proud to accept avoidance. Especially from her. Would she ever see past what was missing to what was still there?

"It's not pretty. But it gets the job done."

She paused in picking up another basket to look him in the eye. "You're back on your feet again. There's nothing ugly about it, Calhoun."

Yeah, *right*. He should enter a beauty pageant. And then Estrada pulled up behind her. *Great*. The other man got out of his Bronco and they exchanged curt nods.

She handed a load to Estrada, who looked none too happy once he realized Bruce lived next door.

Bruce set his basketball on top of an even bigger load and followed the other man inside. "Left at the top of the stairs," he said, directing Estrada toward Mitzi's bedroom.

Bruce reached past Estrada to flip on the light switch for him.

The room looked almost the same as it had when she'd left for the Navy. A lot of blue and white, the school colors. *Pirates of the Caribbean* posters. She'd had a crush on Orlando Bloom. So there were plenty of *The Lord of the Rings* movie posters, too.

Bruce set his load down at the foot of Mitzi's old bed. He knew that bed intimately. Without saying a word he picked up his basketball and walked over to the window that faced his.

Estrada got the message.

But Estrada had a message of his own to deliver. "You know the difference between the Army and the Marine Corps?"

"Marines are first to fight."

Get in. Get it done. Get out.

The Army on the other hand had a hell of a lot more equipment to drag along for the fight.

"When you're long gone, Marine, I'll still be here." Estrada turned heel and left the room.

CHAPTER EIGHT

"WHERE'VE YOU BEEN?" Bruce asked, flipping on the light in the kitchen as his brother tried to sneak in after curfew.

Keith jumped. "Jeez! Scare me, why don't you?"

"Sunday's a school night."

"I was studying," Keith answered irritably. "I have midterms this week." Head down texting, he tried to push past.

Bruce pulled out a chair. "Have a seat." Keith puffed his chest, but dropped his backpack and sat anyway.

Bruce took the chair opposite his kid brother and set Keith's cell phone out of reach.

"I was looking over your SAT and ACT scores," he said, referencing the two college entrance exams Keith had taken earlier in the school year. "You know there is such a thing as a college-educated Marine. I'm willing to talk to you about OCS. ROTC. Annapolis, Naval Academy—"

"Naval Academy?"

"Sailors and Marines are joined at the hip," Bruce offered as way of explanation. "My point is there's a whole world out there. If it seems like I'm coming down hard on you, or on the side of college, it's because I see you making mistakes I made at your age."

"Seriously doubt it," Keith scoffed.

"Care to enlighten me?"

Keith shook his head. "It's nothing."

Clearly it *was* something. With patience Bruce would get it out of him eventually. "I'm here if you need me."

"Yeah, but for how long?" Keith grumbled.

"I'm only a text or an email away."

"It sucks having an older brother who's a freaking hero," he said. "Everybody expects the same out of me and I'm not half as tough."

"I'm no hero."

"You used your own belt as a tourniquet, then picked up your gun and went after those guys that ambushed your convey."

"Where'd you hear that?"

"A corpsman by the name of Henriquez told me *and Dad*. That day we went to Luke's and Freddie's funerals in California. Said you wouldn't let him help you. That you kept yelling at him to keep working on Freddie, even though he was gone and his guts were spilling out."

Bruce hoped to hell Mitzi hadn't heard that story.

"Yeah, well, it's an exaggeration." He did use his belt as a tourniquet. But every Marine and Navy SEAL he'd ever known had been trained to use his web belt or helmet strap for that.

And he did pick up his weapon to help defend their position, but the insurgents who'd fired the RPG were long gone by then.

It wasn't until a week later that the able-bodied members of their team captured the people responsible. Bruce was already at Balboa by then.

Bruce studied his brother from across the table. "Do you think the Marine Corps is going to toughen you up?" That was probably true. "Not everyone needs to be tough."

Keith dropped his gaze to the table. "I just think it's time I grew up and took responsibility."

"Don't be in such a hurry, kid. The Marine Corps will still be there after college. Right now you're a hero on the hardwood. That's plenty."

"I'm not that great a basketball player."

Keith was your average overachiever. He worked hard. When challenged, he worked harder. Sometimes too hard. "You're good enough, Keith. Have some fun. You're only eighteen once."

"You were better. Everyone says so."

"But I wasn't smart enough to take advantage of everything that came my way because of it. If you're having doubts, or you're overwhelmed by your choices, I get it. But you're not being offered scholarships because you suck at basketball. And here's the truth.... You're smarter than me. Everyone thinks so, including me."

Keith attempted a laugh. "You're wrong about that."

Bruce got up from the table, squeezed his brother's shoulders. "I don't think so." He gave him a brotherly pat on the back. "It's late—you've got school tomorrow."

His brother made a hasty retreat from the kitchen as Bruce walked over to the back door, checked the lock and hit the lights. At that moment headlights from a car pulling into the driveway next door streamed across the kitchen wall, then went dark.

He heard two car doors. Lowered voices. Then silence. They must've been kissing good-night.

Three nights in a row, starting Friday night—the night she'd moved back home—Mitzi had gone out with Estrada. Bruce knew what time the other man had picked her up, what time he'd brought her home and the exact length of those three good-night kisses.

He'd had the whole weekend to think about what Estrada had said to him up in Mitzi's bedroom. *When you're long gone, Marine, I'll still be here.*

As much as he hated to admit it, the other man was right.

The bottom line was Bruce didn't deserve her. And she deserved to be happy. Whether that was with Dan or some other man remained to be seen.

Meanwhile, he owed it to Freddie to make sure that man was worthy of his little sister.

Bruce picked up the basketball by the door, flipped the floodlight on and headed outside to level the competition. *"Grunt,"* he called, aiming for the other man's head and, for the third night in a row, spoiling that good-night kiss.

The coach had the reflexes of a natural athlete and caught the ball easily. "What, you're not tired of this game yet, *Devil Dog?"*

"Ground Pounder."

"Jarhead."

"Not tired by a long shot," Bruce said.

Mitzi sighed heavily. "Good night, *boys,"* she said, leaving them to battle it out in the driveway under the floodlights.

The thing Bruce recognized about himself, and it had been that way since high school, was that if there was competition, he stepped up his game. On and off the court.

He couldn't lose what he'd already lost, but he could make the other man work a little harder…a lot harder…at winning her affection.

THE SUN WASN'T EVEN UP when Mitzi pulled into the gravel lot behind the recruiting station on Monday morning to find Henry's empty wheelchair parked beside the Dumpster. She got out of her car and walked up to the bin. They'd first met under similar circumstance.

"Henry, you're going to get yourself crushed one of these days!"

"Pick up ain't until later this afternoon." He peered over the side and she noticed the faded, yellowish bruise on his cheek.

"What *happened* to you?"

She offered him her hand. Despite his disability and limited mobility, he appeared agile enough to crawl around in Dumpsters. It was his getting in and out that scared her.

Refusing to let go of the crumpled McDonald's bag in his hand, he rolled over the side onto his good foot. She helped him down and over to his wheelchair. "Found me a couple of Egg McMuffins."

Who would throw out Egg McMuffins?

"I'm talking about your black eye."

"Some young punks jumped me in the alley Thursday night. Stole my meds."

"Are you all right?" She couldn't bear to think about him living on the street the way he did. It wasn't the first time he'd been robbed.

"Right enough."

"Come on in. I'll fix you a cup of coffee." She unlocked the back door and held it open for him. "And throw that bag away. I'll find you something to eat."

Mitzi dropped her things off at her desk and set about making a fresh pot of coffee. "Have you ever considered moving back into a real apartment?"

"Can't afford nothing."

"There must be some place. What about assisted living? Or subsidized housing?"

"Bah, be dead before I move up on that list."

She opened the cupboards, looking for food. "You could move in with me."

"Shouldn't you be asking one of those young guys?"

She glanced over her shoulder at him. "I meant into the other half of my duplex. It's not quite move-in ready, but I have a contractor over there right now. I could call him and get an estimate on a wheelchair ramp and an accessible bathroom."

What had seemed impulsive at first started to feel right.

"Wouldn't want to put you out."

"You're not putting me out."

"Can't afford much in the way of rent."

"I'm not asking for much."

"Never said I was a charity case."

She pulled out a jar of peanut butter and continued her search for crackers. "Never thought you were." She smiled to herself.

As much as he'd like her, and everyone else, to believe he'd chosen to be homeless, she knew better. He'd been displaced this time after his rent had skyrocketed beyond what he could afford on his fixed income.

She moved aside paper plates and napkins. "I'd like having you next door. We could keep an eye on each other."

"Already have that fella of yours bothering me most nights. Now you're gonna start checking up on me, too."

"Dan?" she asked, surprised they even knew each other.

"The ornery one."

She'd found a roll of crackers to go with the peanut butter and turned to face Henry. "Calhoun?"

"Took those punks out just like Nick Cage. All three of them."

The coffee was just about done. Mitzi got out two cups and cream and sugar while Henry filled her in.

"Next day he called the VA and got me an emergency fill of my meds. We're going back today to pick up my new prescription," Henry finished.

He'd never said a word to her.

She held out the wastebasket. "Okay, hand over the bag."

He scowled at her as he threw it away. She'd seen Calhoun with a McDonald's bag on Friday morning. Those breakfast sandwiches might have been that old.

"What else do you have in your hand?"

"Nothing," he said.

Mitzi continued to hold out the wastebasket. Henry opened his hand to reveal a small black velvet box.

Mitzi caught her breath.

Setting the basket down, she reached for it. "May I see that, please?"

"Why?" Henry pulled back. "Ain't nothing in it." He snapped the lid open to prove it, then closed it again before tucking it away.

Seeing the box empty didn't bring Mitzi the expected relief. Okay, so maybe Calhoun didn't throw the ring out with the box. But maybe he did.

BRUCE COULD SMELL the coffee as he came in through the front door. "Good morning."

"What's so good about it?" Mitzi, in her desert digital uniform, did an about-face and left him standing there.

Henry snickered. "She sure shut you down, Marine."

"At least one of us knows when to shut up, old man," he said pointedly. "You ready to roll?"

Bruce led the way to the green sedan with the

gold Marine Corps recruiting logo parked out back. When it came to loading and unloading the wheelie, he had the drill down this time.

They were going to pick up Henry's meds. But Bruce had also scheduled an appointment for a leg adjustment before this upcoming ski trip and his O-course, just to make sure his new C-Leg was up to the challenge.

He'd run the obstacle course at Camp Pendleton numerous times before leaving San Diego. He could cheat, use a lighter leg designed for running, but he wanted to test the leg he'd most likely be wearing in the field.

Flipping through an old *Stars and Stripes* magazine in the waiting room, he found it hard to concentrate. He kept thinking about Mitzi. The knot-in-gut feeling that he walked into every morning. Were they going to be chatting over coffee or not speaking to each other that day?

One minute she was honoring him with her brother's watch and the next she was handing him back her engagement ring.

Given their history, maybe a clean break wasn't possible. Maybe what they needed first was closure.

"I've been coming here every week for six months—" Henry's raised voice could be heard throughout the waiting room "—and you've been telling me the same thing!"

"I'm sorry, sir," the receptionist said. "We don't have any appointments available today for a new prosthesis fitting. We have an opening six weeks from today, and I can put you on the list for the first available appointment if one should open up sooner."

"More waiting. All I do is—"

Bruce stepped up to the counter. "What seems to be the problem?"

Henry waved him off. "Same as always."

"I was just telling Mr. Meyers I can't get him in today," the receptionist repeated. "But if he would like to put his name on the list…"

"Can you look again, please?" Bruce asked. He'd called at the end of last week and had gotten in no problem.

She entered something into her computer, then shook her head. "I'm sorry."

"Go ahead and give him mine," he offered.

"I can't do that, Gunnery Sergeant," she said. "Mr. Meyers is requesting a new prosthesis. As I've told *him* numerous times," she said, directly to Henry, "the waiting list for the first available appointment really isn't that long compared to the length of time he's been coming in here and demanding to be seen right away."

"How am I supposed to go on a waiting list when I don't have a phone?" Henry grumbled.

"Get him on the schedule for six weeks from

today, and use my cell to call if there's an earlier opening."

"Thank you," she said, relieved.

"You're making this harder than it has to be, you stubborn old goat," he said to Henry.

"For all you know I could be dead in six weeks."

"How many months have you been coming in here demanding to be seen?"

"Bah."

"Don't go anywhere," Bruce said as the old man started to scoot off.

A few minutes later Bruce dragged Henry into the physical therapy room with him. He explained the situation to the doc, who agreed to look at Henry's leg. His problem wasn't just a prosthesis that was older than Bruce. Henry's stump had changed. And the leg was no longer a good fit.

After the examination the doctor excused himself to consult his technician. He came back a few minutes later with a training leg. "I may have a temporary fix. But you're going to have to start walking all over from scratch."

After wrapping Henry's stump with a compression bandage to guard against the expected abrasions of learning to walk again, the doctor had Henry put on a stump sock before slipping on the socket.

Stump socks came in various thicknesses. The

trick was choosing the right one for normal, some-times daily fluctuations, usually water retention. But even the weather could affect the fit. For Bruce his prosthesis was held in place by suction with nothing between the stump and the socket. But with fit and circulation a factor in Henry's case, his socket was held in place by a Silesian bandage.

"How does that feel?" Doc asked, attaching the leg. The old man nodded. "Can you stand?"

Henry couldn't stand on his own, so Bruce supported the vet's frail body while the doctor attempted to adjust the trainer to his height. The gait training leg was little more than an adjustable pole with a foot.

Henry didn't own a right shoe to put on the prosthetic foot. But it was the first time in years that he had had a right leg he could actually stand on. Bruce noted the determined set to the vet's chin as they led him to the parallel bars so he could practice bearing his own weight.

Moving sideways along a single bar was just one beginner exercise. The old man's arms were shaking just from the strain of holding himself up. The doc had him move to his right, off his trainer.

Lift. Step. Plant.

A lot harder than it seemed.

He was able to take a few more with his good left leg in the lead. Those first few steps were as frustrating as they were exciting.

"We'll work on it," Bruce said when he saw the frustration on the weathered vet's face. He was eager to take his first steps—he just wasn't ready.

They helped Henry back to his wheelchair.

Henry left his trainer on. The technician wanted to use parts of his old leg to fashion a new custom leg. The mold for the new fitted socket would be made at his appointment.

Useless as it had become, Henry still had a hard time letting go of his old leg. Eventually the thought of a new leg won out and he gave in.

"You're next," the doc said.

Bruce had thought he'd given up his appointment, but his examination didn't take long. His C-Leg was none the worse for wear. The doctor pronounced him fit and ready to take on the O-course. Skiing. And any other sport he might like to try.

Having stripped down to his jockey shorts without giving Henry's presence a second thought, Bruce was pulling his T-shirt over his head and down past his six-pack abs when Henry saw fit to comment.

"I had a body like that once."

Bruce heard years of regret behind those words, but refused to play to the pity. "Old man," he said, "you never had a body like this."

They both chuckled. Just so long as Henry

realized he had to start taking better care of the one he had. In the mirrors that lined the therapy room Bruce caught a glimpse of the two of them side by side.

"A RAK. And a LAK," Henry said, coming to the same conclusion. "You're a size what, thirteen? Between us we could get by with only one pair of shoes."

"I need both shoes," Bruce said. "And so do you. What do you say we make a quick stop on the way back to the office for a new pair?"

Bruce picked up his uniform pants. As he put them back on he remembered sticking his dive watch into the pocket after Mitzi had given him her brother's. He felt around for it now to see if it was this particular pair of pants. Sure enough. Good thing it was waterproof. He'd done his laundry this weekend.

"What do you need two watches for?" Henry asked.

"I don't." And the keeper was already on his wrist. Knowing how honored he'd felt when Mitzi entrusted him with it there, and that it was never coming off, he said, "Hold out your arm."

Henry complied and Bruce fastened his old watch to the wheelie's wrist. Henry looked it over. "A Luminox. That must be worth something. Sure you don't want to save this for that kid brother of yours?"

"Definitely not." The watch had been a gift from Lucky when Bruce had completed BUD/S training. He did not want to encourage Keith in that direction.

Con artist that Henry was, the *quick* stop for a new pair of shoes turned into a haircut and a shave at a high-end salon where the beauticians wore lingerie.

Lunch at Hooters.

And a trip to the pawnshop.

Bruce was seething when Henry came rolling out of the shop without his watch. "If I'd known you were going to pawn the damn thing—"

"Need the deposit money for my new landlord."

Bruce felt like a complete ass. Of course a roof over the old man's head was far more valuable than an old watch.

Good riddance.

"Remind me—you're going to want this pawn ticket someday." Henry tucked it away into his pack as they headed back to the car.

"Keith doesn't need my old dive watch."

"Never heard one man's trash is another man's treasure?"

Obviously the old man lived by that rule.

All in all, that new pair of shoes cost Bruce about two hundred bucks. And Henry now had more cash than what Bruce would have thought his old Luminox was worth. What else had the old guy pawned?

CHAPTER NINE

"PEACE OFFERING," Calhoun said upon his return to the office.

Mitzi raised an eyebrow as he dropped off Hooters takeout at her desk. "Thank you, I think."

"They have good wings," he said.

"And I thought you went for the breasts and thighs," she said, still seething from Henry finding that ring box in the Dumpster this morning. She didn't know whether to confront Bruce about it or not.

He leaned across her desk. "Henry picked the place. I just went along for the ride."

"I see you got a haircut. Was that Henry's idea, too?"

"As a matter of fact, Henry knows quite the barbershop," he said, whistling his way to his desk.

He was in a chipper mood. He either didn't know or didn't care what they'd found in the trash.

Mitzi got moodier as the afternoon wore on.

The minute she stepped out the back door and

lifted the lid on the Dumpster, she realized she was insane. She pulled herself up and over and into the middle of all that garbage anyway.

It wasn't the ring, she told herself as she sifted through waste-high rubbish. She'd returned his ring. It was his to do with as he pleased. Even throw it away.

She burrowed deeper into the refuse, despite a smell so bad it made her want to gag.

Did sentiment have no value to him at all?

She knew the inscription by heart.

"*Semper Fi,* 09.11.01."

The date, of course, had nothing to do with their engagement—9/11 was the day the twin towers came down. The day Freddie and Bruce enlisted.

Her brother had walked away from the police academy without looking back. Bruce had been a freshman in his first few weeks of college when he'd left basketball, and her, behind.

Near tears, she'd been digging for almost an hour and hadn't found anything. Her hands were as raw as her nerves and her nose was dripping.

Wiping her forearm across her forehead, she had to admit defeat. She was never going to find it. If it was ever even here.

"What are you doing?" Keith stood outside the Dumpster in his warm letterman jacket with his backpack slung over his shoulder.

Mitzi checked her watch. That late already?

Her DEPers would start showing up soon.

"I thought I'd lost something." Her voice had a weariness to it. "Guess I was mistaken. What are *you* doing?" she asked, still inside the Dumpster.

"Bruce said I could come by and work out with the DEPers."

"That's right. I'd forgotten."

"Do you think you could work on changing his mind?"

"That would be up to you." It was one argument she did not want to be in the middle of.

They heard air brakes as a garbage truck pulled into the alley and stopped in back of the building. The driver got out, leaving his door open. "Lady!" he shouted across the parking lot.

"What's your problem? I'm getting out!" she shouted with a defensive shrug. It wasn't as if she hadn't known it was trash pickup day. Desperation had driven her to at least look.

Before the ring wound up in a landfill somewhere.

He got into his truck and she heard that beep, beep, beep warning as he started to back up.

"Can I help you out?" Keith offered.

"I got it," she said, swinging her leg up and pulling herself out. She'd run her fair share of obstacle courses.

The driver checked his mirrors to make sure they were both out of his way. Mitzi took a step back and bowed with a sweeping gesture toward the Dumpster. "It's all yours."

THEY WERE RUNNING along the South Platte River trails.

"Left. Right. Left, right, left!" Bruce called cadence to keep everybody in step. Mitzi ran beside him. His brother and her four DEPers behind them echoed lines.

"Everywhere we go…" He started an old favorite of his from boot camp. "People want to know. Who we are. Where we come from. We come from an island…Parris Island."

"I don't see any Marine recruits back there, Gunny," Mitzi taunted.

"It *ain't* like the Army, at Fort Jackson." He put emphasis on ain't for her benefit. "It ain't like the Navy, down in Florida." He slanted a glance to catch her reaction. She pursed her lips and pushed on. "It ain't no flyboy, over in Texas."

"Whoa, oh. Whoa, oh." The kids were starting to get the hang of it and added their own little spin.

"There ain't no other. Parris Island."

Mitzi nudged him with her shoulder. "Enough, Parris Island." She kept it in cadence. "These kids ain't goin' to South Caroline."

He'd gone to boot camp in Parris Island, South Carolina.

She picked up her pace on the incline and they all had to kick it into gear. Not to be outdone, Bruce pushed her to try to stay even with him.

"What's that smell?" He leaned over to sniff her hair. "Whew, you need a shower there, Chief."

She elbowed him hard in the gut and he took a misstep and had to allow his C-Leg to readjust for a few paces before pulling even again. "Watch where you're swinging those things."

"Trust me, I would have aimed lower if I could."

"If there's something you want to say to me, just say it."

"Go jump in the Platte," she said, stopping them both. She started walking backward, in the direction they'd come from, and shrugged. "There, said what I had to say." She turned and continued walking away.

Keith, followed closely by the SEAL twins, caught up to them and didn't know whether to stop, slow down or turn around and follow Mitzi.

"Round back to the station," Bruce said before going after her. The gamer and the girl used the break in action to stop and catch their breaths.

"Keep walking," Keith said.

It didn't take Bruce long to catch up to her. Mitzi telling him to go to hell, which is how he'd interpreted it, wasn't any worse than having been there. But knowing that she meant it hurt.

"Normally you smell…good."

Like a field of wildflowers on the western slopes. Or a magnolia plantation in South Carolina. Or a cactus in the moonlight. Everywhere he'd ever been had a scent that reminded him of her.

"This isn't about my hair." She crossed her arms.

He figured that.

"I spent the afternoon digging through a Dumpster…."

Because he'd slam-dunked her ring into it?

"Never mind." She reached to scratch her scalp and wound up taking her hair down. "I need a shower. Just…stay out of my way today, Calhoun."

Mitzi pulled into the parking lot at Englewood High School Wednesday afternoon and parked her navy blue sedan as far from the red USMC Hummer as she could get. Every available surface of the monster vehicle was painted with official USMC images. It even had eagle, globe and anchor hubcaps.

The Army arrived in a similar black Hummer. And the Guard rode in with a red, white and blue mural painted on their van.

Annie stepped out of a bright blue sedan not unlike Mitzi's navy blue one. Until recently the Air Force had never had to go looking for recruits. The Navy and Air Force had all the cool high-tech jobs and were a much easier sell to both kids and parents. A bad day on the job for a Navy recruiter was nowhere near as tough as it was for a Marine recruiter.

They were all wearing their service's combat utilities because that was the "cool" uniform. The one that impressed the kids the most.

Mitzi grabbed her box of goodie bags from her trunk and walked into the building with Annie.

"Sucks to be them," Annie said.

This was Mitzi's second Career Day, she knew exactly what the other woman was talking about. They parted ways in the hall where Bruce was setting up tables outside the auditorium.

Career Day was open to colleges, as well. They were each given five minutes to speak to the captive audience. Afterward the kids and their parents were free to roam the halls and stop by their tables for more information.

Colleges went first, followed by the trade and tech schools. The military was lumped together last.

Mitzi used this quiet time to set up her area. She noticed Calhoun slip inside the auditorium to stand near the back. Lack of a college education was one of his big regrets. And she suspected the reason he was so adamant his brother would attend.

Was he gathering information for Keith or for himself? She wondered if he even knew that, with approval, recruiters could attend college during working hours, provided they wore the uniform. Lots of perks with the job.

What was she doing reaching for reasons he should stay? He'd had one very good reason—her. And that wasn't enough. To hell with him.

There was the usual shuffling in the audience as the armed services took the stage. For juniors and seniors attendance was mandatory and a good excuse to miss a half day of classes. Not so for the parents. A few got up to leave because of schedules or in quiet protest. One woman wasn't so quiet.

Spouting her views on what she called the economic draft, the woman was escorted from the building by the police officer on duty at the school. At least no one had pulled the fire alarm or called in a bomb threat. Yet.

Settling into their seats on the stage in the order in which they were speaking—more or less alphabetical—Mitzi sat in the second to last chair, with Calhoun to her right. The Marine Corps' position was always to the right of the Navy.

The Colorado National Guard went first. Followed by Air Force Annie, who could always be counted on for a laugh, and to go over five minutes.

As Mike and Ike did their tag-team routine for the Army, Mitzi shuffled through her index cards. Public speaking was not her thing. Luckily she had a three-minute commercial that would be projected onto the screen behind her and only two minutes to fill.

The polite applause for Mike and Ike faded.

Stepping up to the podium, Mitzi took a deep breath and scanned the audience for a friendly face. She found Dan's and smiled back at him. Challenging herself to work hospital corpsman into her spiel at least four times, she began.

"Good afternoon, I'm Chief Petty Officer Mitzi Zahn. Eight years ago I was sitting where you are today wondering what I was going to do with my life.... I played the snare drum in the school band—" she smiled at Kelly in the crowd "—your basic overachiever.

"College was certainly an option. But I was eager to get out into what I considered the 'real world.'" She supplied air quotation marks for *real world*. "My brother and his best friend had joined the military two years earlier. They seemed to be having fun—I wanted to have some *fun*." Her emphasis on *fun* generated a collective laugh from her audience.

"In reality what they were doing was taking on responsibilities I never dreamed of. The fun came in their love of life and the jobs they were doing. They were both with the SEAL teams at the time. So I walked into the very recruiting station where

I work today and told my recruiter I wanted to be a Navy SEAL.

"Well, he laughed as loud as you're laughing now. Then he told me I couldn't be a Navy SEAL because I was *a girl,* but he could make me a hospital corpsman. I said okay, and signed up for the delayed entry program." She really had been that naive. "A few months later I graduated from high school and shipped off to boot camp followed by hospital corpsman 'A' school.

"At the end of it I watched my fellow corpsmen go on to work with SEALs and Seabees and even Marine Force Recon teams. Of course, they were all *guys.*" She paused again for the laughs. "And while most corpsmen will work within a hospital environment, I knew that wasn't what I wanted. I met with a savvy Navy career counselor and told her my dilemma—I was born with the wrong set of genes.

"She took one look at my file and said, '…I see you were captain of your swim team in high school. I can get you into special ops.' A girl in spec ops— what a concept. I said, 'What do I have to do?' After two years of intensive mental and physical training, I became an AIRR, an aviation rescue swimmer. SAR—search and rescue—is some of the most rewarding work you'll find anywhere.

"As it turned out, my hospital corpsman background proved invaluable, as I later went on to advanced AIRR school for emergency medical training. You're sitting here today with a world of possibilities before you. Let me open your mind to what the United States Navy can do for you. Thank you."

Mitzi finished as the motto for rescue swimmer flashed across the screen behind her: *So Others May Live*. The first of six thirty-second high-octane "Accelerate Your Life" clips began to play. She ended with a low-key favorite of hers called "Navy SEAL Footprints," a night shot of a beach with a cloud-covered moon, waves crashing against the shore.

A wave rolled in and when it rolled out again there were footprints. Another wave washed the footprints away. *You never see the Navy SEALs.*

"I missed 'em. Show it again," a smart-mouth in the back shouted—there was always a smart-mouth in every high school auditorium. When she was in high school, Calhoun had been that guy. He'd have done anything for laughs. Mitzi wasn't in control of the video, but the boys up in the audio/visual booth did run it again.

It was a good lead-in for Calhoun, even though he wouldn't be talking about his time with the SEALs. He was Marine Force Recon through and through. And right now he was a Marine Corps recruiter.

The three and half minutes of Navy commercials

led into three minutes of Marine Corps commercials. She and Calhoun exchanged places.

"They saved the best for last. Normally Marines are first to fight," he said. "I'm Gunnery Sergeant Bruce Calhoun, United States Marine Corps. I won't keep you long, I know you've been sitting for a while, and trust me, I remember how hard those auditorium seats get. I want to talk to you today about what it takes to be a Marine.

"*Semper Fidelis* is more than a motto—it's a way of life. Latin for 'always faithful,' it reminds us of our core values, that Marines are held to a higher standard of honor, courage..."

And commitment.

To the Corps. Mitzi tuned out the rest of his speech.

"Becoming a Marine is a transformation that begins with boot camp where you earn your EGA—eagle, globe and anchor. But it can never be undone.

"We don't accept applications. Only commitments." He ended with a recruiting slogan.

Calhoun might as well have ended with a couple of hoorahs.

He had the kids lining up at his table. And their parents glaring at him.

"Hey," Dan said. He was carrying a rolled paper in his hand.

"Hey, there, handsome. Care for a water bottle?" she asked.

He was wearing his Army uniform today, so she thought it kind of cute when he accepted a Navy water bottle from her.

"I have something for you, too," he said, handing her the document in his hand. "Mike says this is as good as gold to a recruiter."

"What is it?"

"It's a list of all my students who've taken the Armed Services Vocational Aptitude Battery, and their scores. I guess you'll get the official report on Monday through your downtown office. Just don't tell your fellow recruiters I leaked it to you early."

"Wow, Dan. I don't know what to say, except thank you."

"I know it's not candy and flowers, but what do you give a recruiter who has everything—beauty, brains…"

"Blush."

"That was next on my list," he said. "I like making you blush." That's because he had a way of making everything he said sound sexy. Especially when he looked at her through his eyelashes with those sleepy eyes.

It must be his hot Latino blood. She felt her cheeks flame.

"What time should I pick you up Saturday night?"

"Can I meet you there? I have a late-afternoon appointment to get my hair and nails done. And I'm not sure how long I'll be."

"Sounds good to me."

"And while I have you here, what are you doing for Thanksgiving?"

"There's our trip to Vail," he pointed out.

"I meant for dinner," she said. Still a couple weeks away—it was never too early to start planning. So that the kids could spend Thanksgiving Day with their families they'd leave for Vail the Friday morning after Thanksgiving and return on Sunday.

"Oh, you know us bachelors. Probably Denny's."

"No, you have to come by the bowling alley. My dad does this thing every year where he closes for business and opens it up to dinner for the homeless."

"Oh, so now you think I'm the poor homeless guy."

"And friends."

"That sounds kind of nice, actually."

"I'll fill you in on the details as we get closer. But be sure to bring your apron."

A JROTC student stopped to talk to Dan about a homework assignment and wound up asking Mitzi a few questions. Then more students stopped by and she got busy.

When she had a chance to look up, Bruce was behind his table across from hers, with Keith standing in front of it. She couldn't hear them above the general din of the crowded hall, but Calhoun was shaking his head at something Keith said.

Keith stormed off in her direction. "Would you please talk some sense into him for me?"

Mitzi made eye contact with Bruce, who shrugged as if he didn't know what was going on.

Later, as they folded the tables to take back to the station, she asked, "What was that about?"

"The usual."

"Maybe you should just let him enlist."

"Because he shows up for a run every day?"

"Because he obviously wants to." There really wasn't anything else to be said and she hated getting into the middle of it. But she was beginning to see Keith's point. It must be frustrating for him when his brother talked to his friends about joining the Marines.

Bruce picked up their tables to carry them outside.

She followed with their empty, or almost empty, boxes.

"Damn it!"

She saw it when he did—his USMC mobile had been egged.

"Eggs aren't going to do that much damage to the paint job in the middle of winter," she said.

Calhoun was already scanning the parking lot for the vandals. Mike stood by his vehicle arguing with an angry parent. It looked as if the Army's Hummer had also been egged. And the heavyset woman with the egg carton wasn't even trying to hide the fact that she'd done it. She looked like the lady who'd been escorted from the auditorium.

Calhoun set the folded tables up against his Hummer and went over to Mike. Mitzi set her boxes down, slower to follow. If this woman was intent on causing trouble, someone should just get the school officer.

"You've got no business talking to my kid!" the woman was screaming at Mike.

"Ma'am, please." Bruce stepped into the middle of it. "Just get in the Hummer, Mike," he said. Ike was already trying to haul Mike off. Between the two of them they got him into the car.

The woman continued to rant at the Army until they drove off. Then she rounded on Bruce.

"What business do you have coming to my son's school and selling him a load of crap?"

"With all due respect, ma'am," Bruce said with complete calm, "this is a public school."

"Where you target kids too young and too naive to know any better! You're no better than a pimp."

"Don't you dare talk to him like that!" Mitzi stepped into the woman's face. Bruce put a restraining hand on her shoulder, but she shook him off. "This man gave his leg for your right to stand there and call him names."

She took advantage of the woman's shocked silence to snatch the egg carton from her. When faced with the little spitfire, the bigger woman backed off long enough for Bruce to drag Mitzi away. "I was just getting started," she said.

"I can see that. You know, you don't always have to come to my rescue. In fact, I'd prefer it if you didn't."

"I'm sorry," she said, stunned. "I wasn't aware you felt that way."

She stopped, while he continued toward his Hummer. She'd had just about enough of him lately.

The first egg hit him between the shoulder blades and stopped him in his tracks. He turned, and the look on his face was priceless. "And this one," she said, picking out the last egg, "is for throwing my engagement ring into a Dumpster." She hurled it at him with the full force of her pent-up anger. "*Semper fi,* Marine."

"SHOULD I DUCK?" Bruce asked, stepping out of their bathroom/locker room with wet hair and in clean combat utilities.

Mitzi looked up from the paper in her hand. "You need to see this."

Keith's name was on the ASVAB list.

Which meant he'd taken the Armed Services Vocational Aptitude Battery. Army was listed as the branch of service for which he'd tested, but the test was good for all branches. Mike was listed as the recruiter.

"It doesn't mean anything," she said. "Other than he took the test. He's not committed to any one branch of the service at this point. Or at all."

Unless it was already too late.

Ninety-six out of a hundred was a hell of a good score. Too good for a ground pounder. Right now Bruce just wanted to punch something. Or someone.

"Bruce," Mitzi warned as he headed next door. She hurried to keep up with him.

"Mike, what the—" He cut himself off when he saw there were kids present. "Can I speak with you?"

"Sure." Mike had the nerve to look as if he didn't know what this was about. Bruce led the way to the back lot.

"You tested my kid brother?"

Mitzi put herself between them.

"Look, Calhoun, before you go throwing that first punch, I tested all the JROTC kids. They get extra credit for it. I haven't even spoken to him yet. Not that I'm not going to," Mike said straight up.

Every recruiter in the district would be calling that list.

Some of them as slick as used car salesmen. Now they all had his brother's information.

And they knew he was interested and he wasn't just another cold call.

"Are we cool?" Mike asked.

"No, we're not cool," Bruce snapped.

Mike exchanged looks with Mitzi before returning inside. Bruce turned toward their own back door and went to sit on the fire stairs. He put his head in his hands.

"He didn't do anything wrong," she said.

He didn't know if she was talking about Mike or Keith at this point. In either case she was right. "I know."

"You need to talk to Keith before someone else does."

He knew that, too.

BRUCE ENTERED THE OFFICE on Thursday morning behind schedule after a staff breakfast downtown to mark the Marine Corps' birthday.

Mitzi paused in her career-counseling session with a young woman. "You have someone waiting for you."

That was a switch. She hadn't said more than

two words to him since Monday. After he'd committed that major faux pas—throwing her ring away where she could find it.

Had she found it? How did she know to look?

According to those bridal magazines, it was his to do with as he pleased. And that meant forgetting he'd ever bought the damn thing. But if she'd wanted it, for whatever reason, why hadn't she just kept it?

As far as he was concerned she'd thrown it away first.

Bruce didn't see anyone waiting for him at his desk. "Where?" he asked.

"In the bathroom."

Bruce went to pour himself a cup of coffee while he waited for his first hot prospect to get out of the head. Unfortunately that gave him time to think about how he'd tortured himself, thumbing through those magazines she'd left behind. Seeing the wedding dresses she'd flagged for their wedding and her comments on each one.

So did a different prospective groom mean a different dress? Or same dress, different groom?

A question better left unanswered.

The bathroom door opened and Bruce looked up to find the coward from the alley. He set his coffee aside.

"Leave now or I call the police," Bruce said quietly.

The kid extended a prescription bottle he'd been palming. "I wanted to return these. I thought the old guy might need them...."

Bruce took it. "Okay, you've returned them." Bruce rounded his desk and locked up the meds.

The kid still wasn't moving. "What does a guy have to do to join the Marines?" he asked, looking around nervously.

"Oh, no, we're not going there. I don't talk to druggies. Or thieves."

"I don't do drugs."

"Not even a little weed?"

"I can pass a piss test."

"That's not what I asked," Bruce said.

"Look," the kid said, "I moved out of my cousin's place because of the drugs. And the dealing. I got nowhere to go since my mom's boyfriend moved in with her."

Bruce hitched up his pant leg, sat on the corner of his desk and folded his arms across his body. He knew how intimidating he looked. He nodded toward the nearest chair opposite him.

It had taken guts to walk in here. Maybe he was worth saving. "What's your name?"

"George," he said, using the Spanish pronunciation for his name.

"Got any dependents that you know of, George?"

"No." He shook his head.

"Don't waste my time if you're illegal. You have to be here legally to enlist."

"I was born here! Third-generation American," George said, dropping the street-tough accent.

"That's good, because I'm going to need a birth certificate. And a high school diploma or equivalent."

"Will a GED work?"

Bruce nodded. Proof of a General Educational Development would do. "And I'm gonna need you to take two tests. A drug test," he said, counting off with his thumb and then his forefinger, "and the ASVAB—Armed Services Vocational Aptitude Battery test. If it looks like you qualify, we'll talk."

He started the kid on a practice test in the back room while he stepped into the bathroom to flush Henry's meds down the toilet. Pouring them out into his hand, he took a deep breath. Good ol' OxyContin.

He'd quit the narcotics cold turkey the day she'd left. Mostly because he didn't want to remember how good it felt to have her all over him while he was high on painkillers. Of course, then he'd self-medicated for a while. Bingeing on alcohol.

But Lucky and Cait had been there to knock some sense into him. Cait, being a pharmacist, had talked to his doctor about alternatives. They'd come up with Neurontin, an anticonvulsant drug that blocked the traumatized and severed nerves in his stump from sending pain signals to his brain. Doctors were starting to use it to treat the very real phenomenon known as phantom pain.

Once the pain was gone, he'd gotten serious about rehabbing his body. And he didn't even need the meds anymore.

"What are you doing?" Mitzi asked from the doorway.

He saw her concern and realized what it looked as if he was doing. "They're not mine. They're Henry's and I'm flushing them down the toilet."

"You can't flush medicines down the toilet. It gets into the water system and back into the drinking water."

It would have been better if George hadn't brought the drugs in with him. "Yeah, well, just this once."

"Is that one of the boys—" Realization dawned. "You need to turn those over to the police."

Bruce couldn't do that without sending his first prospective recruit off to jail. He was walking a fine line here. He justified it by telling himself he was taking a kid and drugs off the street.

"Oops." He flushed the evidence. She shook her head, letting him know he'd disappointed her again. "He's a good kid. And he deserves a second chance," he said in his own defense.

George passed the practice test with flying

colors and Bruce started the enlistment paper-work. Because he was over eighteen and no longer in high school there was no need for a delayed enlistment.

Bruce made arrangements to pick up the boy the next day and take him downtown for official testing. He'd have George sworn in and shipped out before George's mother had a chance to kick out her boyfriend.

"I'm sorry," Mitzi was saying to the young woman she'd been in session with all morning. "I can't enlist you if you're a single parent. I wish you'd been up front about your son."

"Please," the young woman said. "We're living with my grandmother. She can take care of him while I'm in boot camp. That's not a problem. I want a better life for him."

"Really there's nothing I can do," Mitzi said.

"I'll do anything," she pleaded. "Take any job." She looked to him for help.

"What I've told you goes for any branch of service," Mitzi said drily.

Bruce handed the young woman a tissue. "All you need is a marriage certificate."

"If I had one of those I wouldn't need to enlist."

She was young. And pretty. And desperate.

"I might know a guy," he said. Mitzi's jaw dropped as he scribbled directions on the back of his business card. "Lives in Wyoming. Doesn't have a phone. He's angry at the world right now. But he might marry you on paper. If just to get back at Uncle Sam." He handed her the card. "What's your name?"

"Angela," she said.

"Come back after you've talked to him."

"That's illegal!" Mitzi accused as soon as Angela was out the door.

"Nothing illegal about it."

"Unethical, then," she said. "Not only that, you stole a recruiting prospect out from under me."

"She's a single mom. You couldn't put her in," he said. "You're just mad because you didn't think of it."

"Well, that's the difference between you and me, Calhoun. I'd never tell a young woman to get married in order to enlist. As if she's coming back with a marriage license. Hatch is scarred inside and out after Iraq. And you didn't even tell her he's as likely to shoot her for trespassing as marry her."

"We'll see," he said smugly. The afternoon mail arrived shortly after that to wipe the smugness from his face. "Mitz, I have a favor to ask."

"Says the man who stole my recruit."

"She's not worth fighting over." The military still wanted young men, ages eighteen to twenty-four.

"So why'd you bother?"

"I'm a sucker for a sob story. I'm hoping you'll be, too, once you hear mine."

"Now you've got me curious."

"Burn this." He handed her the unopened envelope. "So I can say I never saw it."

"This is an invitation to the Marine Corps Birthday Ball." The USMC birthday logo made it obvious to her, as well. "Looks like you made it onto the late invite list." She opened it and read, "Dress uniform required. Attendance *mandatory*."

She handed him the two tickets.

Great, he could ask his mom.

"Better get that dress uniform to the dry cleaner and put a rush on it. Today may be the Marine Corp's birthday, but the party is this Saturday night. Happy birthday, Calhoun."

SITTING BESIDE HER DAD on the couch, Mitzi reached for a handful of popcorn. "Would you like to go see *The Nutcracker* this year? We haven't been in a while."

"I love the ballet," Nora Jean said from the other side of the couch. "Especially that one."

Nora Jean was Luke's mom. And Lucky and Bruce's stepmom.

Mitzi's dad and Nora Jean attended a grief support group together. Mitzi had gone once, and that was enough to know it wasn't for her. But until she'd moved back in with her father she'd had no idea how entrenched the woman was in his life.

"Sure, we can do that," he said, only half listening as he surfed through the channels for a movie they could all agree on.

"I'm sorry, Nora Jean," Mitzi said sweetly. "I only have the two tickets for opening night. And they're sold out."

"That's too bad," Nora Jean said.

"We could all go another night," her father suggested. "You could invite that fella of yours along."

"Oh, no, Fred. Mitzi already has the tickets. Date night with your daughter is important. You and I can go see *The Nutcracker* another time."

Bah, humbug. So her poor dad wouldn't have to sit through it twice, she gave up her tickets. "Take Nora Jean, Dad." Nothing like being the fifth wheel on your own couch. Your own dad's couch anyway. Mitzi got up to microwave her *own* bag of popcorn. She was tired of sharing. "You two watch whatever you want. I think I'm going to watch TV up in my room." Instead Mitzi grabbed her microwave popcorn and several movies from the console, then headed outside to her dad's minivan.

All because Nora Jean was intent on spoiling their father-daughter tradition. And because she herself was being selfish in excluding the other woman.

Her poor dad. Mitzi climbed into the back of the minivan for a good sulk.

"What's Mitzi doing in the van?" Bruce peered out the kitchen window as he helped his mother load the dishwasher. "She's been out there a half hour now."

"Why don't you go ask her?" his mother suggested.

"I'm not going to ask."

It was none of his business.

Bad enough he had to work in the same office. Sleep with a bedroom window facing her temporary one. These glimpses into her life were hell. He didn't imagine his physical fitness test would be before the holidays. But he hoped it would be right after the New Year.

Still staring out the window, he rinsed another plate and handed it to his mother.

"Bruce," she said, recalling his attention. "Do you remember carrying Mitzi piggyback all the way to school her first day of kindergarten? She worshipped the ground you walked on from that moment on."

Shutting off the water, he flung the dish towel over his shoulder and leaned back against the counter. *Way to take my mind off Mitzi.* Freddie had tried to ditch her and she'd stopped to cry. *Mom's going to be mad at you, Freddie, if you lose me!*

Her mom was sick, and he felt sorry for her, so he'd gone back for her. "Her red cowgirl boots were too small and pinched her feet."

"She'd outgrown them that summer." His mom chuckled. "But still insisted on wearing them everywhere." She closed the dishwasher. "That stubborn little girl has loved you for a long time. But it was always going to be a long fall from that pedestal, Bruce."

Well, he'd certainly hit bottom.

"What are you doing Saturday night?" he asked, for a change of subject.

"Sorry, son. I have a date." She shrugged. "Don't forget to take out the trash," his mother said, turning out the light.

Bruce reached under the sink and found a half-empty bag of trash and the excuse he needed to head outside in his T-shirt and pajama pants. He crossed to the Zahns' drive and ducked into the back of their minivan on the driver's side, sliding the door shut behind him. "What's up?"

It took him only a few seconds to assess the situation. Mitzi was huddled in a blanket on the bench seat with a box of tissues. Dry-eyed, but staring at the small screen.

Home movies. This wasn't good.

"Move over," he said, making her sit to one side. "What are we watching?"

"Christmas."

The Christmas he and Freddie had gotten those sticky-dart guns—that didn't stick—in their stockings. There was Freddie in his Spider-Man pajamas, hamming it up for the camera while pretending to die onscreen. And here she was watching it.

Not good. He pried the remote from her hand.

"Hey, I was going to watch a movie."

"It's freezing out here," he said. "Wouldn't you be more comfortable inside?"

"No, I would not. My dad's making out with your stepmother," she said.

"Which one?"

"Pick one."

"For the record, I don't consider either of them my stepmother." It wasn't as if they'd helped raise him. Or were even still married to his dad.

"I meant pick a movie." She directed him to the stack at his feet. "I gave up *The Nutcracker* tickets for Nora Jean," she sulked.

He chose *Con Air* and loaded the DVD player. "Oh, come on, Mitz." He nudged her. "Your dad's been alone a long time. Didn't you ever think about him getting married again?"

"I always thought it would be Audrey."

"Audrey? From the bowling alley?"

"Exactly. She's been in his life so long he doesn't even notice her anymore."

"I'm sure he notices," he said, not sure of any such thing as he hit the play button. Except how small the backseat of the van seemed. The intro started rolling and she tossed a corner of the blanket over his lap. The title came up on screen.

"Do you remember the Cinderella Twin Drive-In?" she asked. "I think we saw this movie there before they tore it down."

He'd thought about it the minute he hit Play.

Her thigh brushed his good one and he swallowed hard. To think, he and Freddie used to make fun of guys with minivans.

She offered him some popcorn. "Make a move and the bunny gets it," she said, borrowing a phrase from the movie.

He'd had the moves back then.

MITZI WAS FINISHING some paperwork at her desk on Friday when Keith walked in. "Don't you have class?"

"Veterans Day," he said.

Duh. Bruce had taken Henry to downtown Denver for the parade and had a few other things scheduled for the day.

"Sure, have a seat," she invited. "Bruce isn't here."

"No, I know." He sat across from her. "I wanted to talk to you about something."

"Is it about the ASVAB? Did Bruce give you a hard time last night?"

"Sort of, but not really. I've kind of changed

my mind about joining the Marines." He couldn't seem to keep his foot still. He picked up a pencil from her desk and drummed it against his palm. "I just turned in a midterm report on the Battle of Iwo Jima."

She sat back, confused about where this was going.

"You know that photo of the Marines raising the flag on Mount Suribachi? Only five of them were Marines. One was a Navy Hospital Corpsman. Bruce said the Navy and Marines were joined at the hip. And yesterday you mentioned being a corpsman before you became a rescue swimmer."

"Nice to know somebody was listening."

"How can I enlist in the Navy and serve with the Marines?"

"Keith," she said, "let's wait until Bruce gets back and we'll talk to him together. If it's the medical field you're interested in, I helped your friend Kelly—"

"Heather's pregnant," he blurted. "I'm the father. I mean, I'm going to be a father."

"Oh, Keith," Mitzi said, reaching across the desk to cover his trembling hand. "Have you talked to your parents?"

He shook his head. "Nobody yet. Except you, I mean."

"You and Heather need to talk to both your parents. If you don't want to talk to them alone, talk to one of your brothers first and have them there with you."

"Yeah, right. Like Bruce wouldn't have a fit worse than Dad.'

"Lucky's a father—"

"I don't need him sticking up for me. I know what I have to do. If you're not going to help me, I'm going to find another recruiter who will."

CHAPTER TEN

A LIGHT SNOW FELL outside the Sheraton Denver Downtown on the night of the Marine Corps Birthday Ball. Standing under the covered drive, wearing his dress blues, Bruce checked his watch again—1800 hours sharp. Five more minutes. That was it.

Although mid-November seemed early for holiday lights, there were signs of the upcoming season everywhere. And now that the valet station behind him had quieted down after a rush of guests, he could hear the ringing bells on the corner.

A white Lexus with the state's Marine Corps plates turned into the circular drive. An attendant rushed forward to open the passenger door and another to take the keys from Lieutenant Colonel Avari.

Snapping to attention, Bruce held his white-gloved salute until the colonel returned it. Bruce stepped to the front door and opened it for the district commander and his wife.

"Thank you, Marine." The colonel glanced at his name tag. "Party's about to start. Waiting on the date?"

"Yes, sir."

"Let me guess. Getting her hair and nails done?"

Colonel Avari's wife took a jab at him with her beaded handbag.

"She should be here any minute, sir."

After the colonel and his wife were inside, Bruce checked his watch *again*. Then he paced toward the bell-ringing wheelie on the corner.

"Got you working as a doorman, I see," said the familiar gruff voice.

"Bell ringer."

"I volunteer." Henry acted insulted.

"Same here."

"Difference is you get paid for your volunteer work." Henry rang his bell and Bruce took the hint, pulled out his wallet and dropped a five into the pot.

Henry cleared his throat. Bruce reached for another five. Henry didn't like that any better, so Bruce pulled out a ten and added both to the pot. Apparently twenty bucks was good enough, because the old man stopped with the throat clearing.

"Wouldn't want to break you," he said, adjusting the wool blanket in his lap.

"You're a real pal." Though said with a heavy dose of sarcasm, Bruce was pretty sure Henry knew he meant it.

He'd taken Henry to the Veteran's Day parade on Friday. And to the VA's annual Stand-Down for homeless vets event at Denver's National Guard armory that morning—where the old man had picked up that blanket and a pair of boots. Regular military were encouraged to hand down their old items, while the VA made sure homeless vets got military ID cards and signed up for services.

Though Bruce would have liked to believe there weren't that many Gulf War and Iraq and Afghanistan vets homeless, he'd seen plenty of them downtown today.

"Look up or you'll miss the show," his pal said.

Bruce scanned the Sixteenth Street Mall.

Gathering her skirts to her knees, Mitzi stepped off the free mall shuttle on the opposite corner and ran the short distance to the hotel. She carried a backpack and wore combat boots and a bomber jacket with her formal gown.

Just as she had on prom night. She'd called it her *Buffy the Vampire Slayer* prom dress. Because he'd said she'd be better off wearing boots than slippers if she was going to be dancing with him.

Bruce squared his shoulders. Her beeline to the circle had bypassed their corner altogether.

"Well," Henry said, "what are you waiting for now?"

The answer should have been obvious as she lowered her skirts and slowed to a walk. "Sorry I'm late," he heard her say breathlessly as she walked up to Estrada.

What the hell was he doing here?

In Army dress blues, no less. This wasn't *his* ball.

"You just gonna stand there looking stupid?" Henry growled at him. "I sure as hell wouldn't stand down while some other fella tried to steal my girl."

"She's not *my girl*." He was her past. This other man was her future. "Not that it's any of your damn business, old man."

Henry waved him off with a ring of his bell.

A taxi and two other vehicles pulled around to the drive. His party had arrived.

"WHAT'S *SHE* DOING HERE?" His aunt Dottie appeared to be more interested in what was going on over her shoulder than at their table. Sitting across from his aunt, Bruce had a better view, but the same question.

She had turned in her bomber jacket and boots at the coat check. Though her ball gown shimmered silver and not white, it looked too much like one of those dresses in the bridal magazines she'd dumped on him.

The heart-shaped bodice. The backless halter. Her bare shoulders.

Estrada used every excuse to touch her. And who could blame him?

Bruce could.

Tonight she wore her hair half-up, in soft curls. With tiny silver flowers in a random pattern that made him want to pluck them even though they weren't real.

Pluck them. And let her hair down.

"Mitzi helped with the Toys for Tots drive last year," Lucky said, settling into his seat between Cait and Bruce. "I put her on the invitation list as a thank-you."

So he had Lucky to thank.

His brother shrugged an apology.

"I thought I saw Mitzi at the beauty shop," his mother commented. Hair and nails being the reason they were sitting at the back of the room. "She looks very pretty tonight. Her dress reminds me of the one she wore to your senior prom. Don't you think so, Bruce?"

Shoot me now.

"So that's the infamous Mitzi?" Cait, looking radiant in her evening dress, hadn't been around long enough to hear all the family gossip. But she'd heard enough. "She's in the Navy, right? Why isn't she in uniform?"

Dottie snorted. "I think she should be, but she doesn't have to be."

"You would know," John said.

"Military women have the option to dress up," his mother said, softening his aunt's answer. The two female vets at their table wore cocktail dresses. Neither had stayed in long enough to retire from the service.

John had retired a gunny and wore his uniform proudly. As did Lucky and their father, Big Luke, who was somewhere—schmoozing—with the brass. Mitzi was hardly the only Navy in a room full of Marines, but most of the others were high-ranking courtesy invites.

An admiral. A couple of captains.

Their full dress white and dinner dress white uniforms stood out in a sea of blue. A Navy chaplain in a Marine uniform was a little harder to spot. And there were probably a couple of corpsmen and chaplain's yeomen in the crowd. Navy personnel serving with the Corps had the option of wearing the Marine Corps uniform as long as they conformed to the stricter standards of grooming.

Estrada stood out in his Army dress blues.

"Why didn't you bring a date, Bruce?" Dottie asked.

Please let this night end.

Bruce had asked his mom, and that's how he'd found out the whole family was going. His aunt had come with his father, so that left him the odd man out. "Smart boy," Big Luke Calhoun said, finally joining them. "Keeping his options open like his old man."

Some options. This was a landlocked state.

The two hundred or so guests were mostly retired or reserves with spouses. Even so, the men here tonight outnumbered the women two to one. The handful of single women his age had dates. A couple of the women he saw in uniform might appreciate his asking them to dance for appearances' sake, but they weren't likely to be ringing each other's bells tonight.

"Gentlemen," his father said, "shall we get these lovely ladies something to drink?"

THE MUSIC WAS SUBDUED for the sake of conversation. Mitzi wasn't much for mingling tonight. She'd had a couple of days' warning when Bruce got his invitation. But she'd accepted her invitation *before* Calhoun's return.

And now wished she hadn't.

Her date would be lucky to make it through the night without a few verbal clashes disparaging his uniform. Head high, Dan didn't seem to mind the impolite stares. Most of them coming from one person at the Calhoun table, a couple rows behind them.

"It doesn't look as if anyone else is going to be joining us this evening," Dan commented on the four empty chairs.

"More champagne for the rest of us." Dale Adams, a navy recruiter from the Littleton office, reached for one of the four bottles. Though he'd served as a corpsman in Iraq, he wore his Navy crackerjack uniform to the ball tonight.

Liz Adams smacked his hand and made him put it back. "That's for the toast." Dale's lovely wife was pregnant with their first child.

As far as Mitzi knew, Keith hadn't told his family about Heather's pregnancy. Or his plans. She was processing his enlistment paperwork out of the Littleton office to avoid the inevitable confrontation.

They'd actually talked at some length before she'd agreed to enlist him. Not that Calhoun would understand.

"You might want to hurry, Estrada," Adams said. "Bar closes in fifteen minutes."

"You'll need your tickets. There's a two-drink limit at the open bar," Liz volunteered. "He's already put away his two and mine." She patted her baby bump.

Adams leaned over and kissed her. "That's how

they keep all these Marines in line until after the speeches."

"Who's going to keep you in line?" Liz asked.

Mitzi dug the tickets out of her beaded handbag.

Her manicured nails had been painted a soft lavender and Dan kissed the back of her hand as she handed the tickets to him. "What would you like?"

She looked into his dark brown eyes, and he smiled. Though she hadn't said it, he knew what she was thinking. He looked mighty fine in that uniform tonight. With his saber at his side.

"They don't have anything fruity," Liz apologized, as if it was her personal responsibility.

"Rum and Coke. Seagram's Seven and Seven," Mitzi said. "Whatever, is fine."

Adams joined Dan in line to keep him company.

"They'll be gone awhile," Liz said.

"Looks like it," Mitzi agreed. "When's your baby due?" That kept the other woman engaged for a while.

Liz segued to the story of how she met her husband in line at the grocery store before stopping to take a breath. "So where did you pick up your date?"

"School."

"College?"

"High school." Her high-school declaration was followed by shocked silence. Mitzi knew she looked young. At twenty-six she was still carded. But not *that* young. "I'm not *in* high school."

"Whew!" Liz lowered her voice to a conspiratorial tone. "It's just that there was this recruiter out of the Englewood office…"

"Yeah, that's not him. Dan's a teacher at Englewood High School."

"What'd I do?" he asked, setting down two light and two dark drinks.

"Mitzi was just telling me how you two met."

"High school," he said.

"God, I miss high school," Adams said, sitting down with something presumably nonalcoholic for his wife.

"Dan!" Mitzi noticed the wet stain on his jacket. "What happened?"

"Nothing. Just club soda," he said. "Got bumped in line."

Nothing. Funny how they both looked up and over at Calhoun at the same time.

AT SOME POINT NEAR the end of the evening, after the cash bar opened up and the dancing commenced, Bruce found himself alone at the table. Leave it to his father to sniff out the only single gal in the room—half his age, and a pretty Marine to boot.

His aunt wasn't doing that badly herself. Of course, the odds were in her favor. And Dottie was a no-pressure dance partner. Her fiancé had died in Vietnam and she'd vowed never to marry.

Huh, that would make Henry and his aunt about the same age... *Nah.* Henry would have to clean up his act before Bruce would ever make that introduction. Besides, his aunt was leading a retired major around the dance floor in a lively two-step at the moment. And even if Henry managed to walk again at his age, he'd likely never recoup enough to dance again.

Then again, he was a feisty old goat.

Bruce gave up on matchmaking and went back to his only other form of entertainment for the evening.

With so many empty chairs he had a clear view of the other man leaning over to place a kiss on Mitzi's bare shoulder. A little higher on her collarbone and he'd have her melting in his arms. Estrada whispered something to her.

Mitzi's eyes brightened as he took her by the hand and led her to the dance floor.

Bruce clenched his jaw. Time to go home.

He really wasn't having much fun anymore.

Halfway to the door one of her favorite Lady Antebellum songs came on—at least it had been one of her favorites. "Need You Now." He turned around.

Bruce strode up to the dance floor and tapped Estrada on the shoulder. The man stumbled to a stop and looked at Bruce over his shoulder.

The tap on the shoulder. A time-honored tradition. Bruce dared Estrada to refuse him. Apparently the other man decided the next three minutes of the song weren't worth a black eye or a loose tooth and stepped aside with a curt nod.

"That was rude." She turned to leave.

He took her hand. Wrapping his arm around her waist, he pulled her close. She tensed as he began to move them around the floor.

"An amputee walks into his doctor's office for a prosthesis fitting. 'Doc, will I be able to dance on this leg?' 'Yes,' the doctor says. 'Good, 'cause I never could before.'"

"*Lame,* Calhoun."

In partners dancing there were no equals—one must be the lead and the other must follow.

His instructor had obviously never tried to dance with Mitzi while she was angry. But Bruce now understood what the woman meant when she'd said exploring the limits of the lead/follow relationship made partners dancing an exciting sport.

Ballroom dancing was not for sissies.

It had taken him months to learn the basic steps. He'd done it for one reason. Let her figure it out.

"You're dancing?" It was a question and a statement in one.

"I though *we* were dancing," he said.

"I just meant you've been taking lessons," she said as they traveled around the floor. The silver dress brought out the violet in her eyes, still bright with anger. And dare he hope, amazement?

"Therapy," he admitted.

"But how? I mean, how does it work, your leg?" She looked embarrassed to be asking, but he didn't mind the question. Or her curiosity.

The layers of her skirt swirled around the red pinstripe of his blue dress pants as he whirled her around to show off one of his fancier moves. "The computer chip in my knee allows for fifty corrections per minute. And adapts to movement."

His dance instructor had three rules. Number one: in improvised dancing the lead was responsible for choosing the steps to suit the music.

The tension between them increased and they moved even closer. Dancing was all about the non-verbal connections and cues. Their bodies, at least, remembered how to communicate.

"As I recall, you had two left feet."

"Now I have four." He'd been wheelchair-bound when she'd left San Diego. But since then he'd gone through his trainer. A latex-covered piece of hardware with lifelike painted hairs. And the experimental leg that put a spring in his step for basketball.

And now his C-Leg.

She didn't get the joke. How could she? She hadn't been there for any of them. He'd seen to that.

Mitzi took the backlead around a guy rocking a wheelchair with a woman in his lap, then gave Bruce back the lead once the danger was past.

Rule number two: for collision avoidance both lead and follow watch each other's backs.

"Careful," he said when she resisted a movement and tried to take the lead from him again. They stubbed toes and he narrowly avoided stepping on hers. He used it as an excuse to hold her even closer. "Maybe you should have kept those boots on."

He could see by the look in her eye that she remembered arriving in boots this evening. But that she also remembered his comment from years ago. "Don't say I didn't warn you," he whispered in her ear. "I'm not that light on my feet."

"At least you won't feel it if I step on your toes."

Their song ended too soon and Lady Gaga's "Poker Face" started, reminding him he might have stolen a dance, but her night would end in another man's arms. "I still have some feelings left, Chief," he said, pulling back. "Try not to crush them."

He escorted her back to Estrada.

Rule number three: to recover from miscommunication, never stop dancing.

MITZI LIKED LADY GAGA, and she and Dan stayed out on the dance floor for the next three fast songs. As long as she didn't slow down, her mind didn't dwell on that one slow dance with Calhoun. Not too much.

When the DJ slowed the music again, Dan got tapped on the shoulder. Again.

"Oh, come on, Calhoun!" he said.

"It's not Bruce," Mitzi said, somewhat surprised to find another Marine standing there.

And again. And on it went until Dan left the dance floor in frustration. Mitzi would have followed, but she didn't have a good excuse for leaving the chaplain without a partner.

BRUCE HADN'T LEFT after all. He was having way too much fun. Estrada crossed over to him with a beer in his hand. "I suppose you had something to do with this."

"Wish I'd thought of it." Bruce leaned back against an empty table and saluted the other man's patience with club soda.

He might have started it, but he certainly hadn't orchestrated it. They stood side by side, watching the line form for a dance with Mitzi.

Obviously torn between hurting her date's feelings and being rude to the dateless men asking her to dance, she kept glancing at Estrada. And subsequently him.

There were a couple of times when they made eye contact that Bruce wanted to believe it was him she was seeking. After several songs of saying nothing, Bruce set his empty glass down on the table and straightened. "Anytime you want to take this conversation outside to the alley, just let me know."

"Oh, I'll do that."

"I'M SO SORRY," Mitzi apologized as soon as she was able to make her way back to Dan at their table. "Do you want to get out of here?"

"Sounds good to me," he said, pulling her close for a kiss.

Dale Adams knocked into them as he returned to the table. "Sorry," he slurred.

"Come on, Pooh Bear," Liz said. "Time for bed."

"Can I call you a cab?" Dan asked.

Liz waved him off. "We have a room in the hotel. But I wouldn't mind help getting him there."

"Absolutely," Dan said.

Mitzi and Liz stopped at the coat check for their things, while Dan tried to keep a drunken sailor headed in a straight line.

"There goes my night of romance," Liz said. "He doesn't let loose often. Just when he knows we don't have to drive."

They caught up with Dan at the elevator. Liz

punched in their floor number for the ride up. "Lot of pressure with a recruiting job," she said with a sigh.

"A little bit," Mitzi agreed.

"He's always wishing he was back in Iraq with his Marines." Liz tried to hide the fact that her eyes were welling up.

Mitzi wanted to smack Dale Adams upside his head. She met Dan's gaze across Adams's slumped body. He winked as if to say *I'm not going anywhere*.

"To the left, off the elevator," Liz said.

They delivered the couple to their room, saw to it they were settled inside, then headed back down the hall to the bank of elevators. Mitzi held an unopened bottle of champagne Liz had wrestled out of her husband's hands.

"Alone at last." Dan pulled her back against his chest and pushed the button to take them to the bridge. As with many sprawling luxury hotels, this elevator to the tower didn't go all the way to the lobby.

Mitzi smiled up at him as she took off her heels and dropped three inches. Tonight could have been a disaster for a sixth date. And would have been if Dan had been a lesser gentleman.

An hour into their very first date, after it was clear there was chemistry, he'd said, "When can I see you again?"

She'd mentioned the tickets to tonight's ball, and he'd said yes. Then she'd asked him to the bowling alley for a midweek date and he'd asked her out three nights in a row last weekend.

In between there'd been coffee, lunch, meeting up with friends. More than six dates, really.

If not a test of his courage, tonight had certainly been a test of his intent. Should she have thought to get a hotel room? Should she be suggesting it now?

She didn't have so much as a toothbrush or a change of clothes in her backpack. And a couple weeks wasn't long to be dating. But that wasn't the hilt of his saber pressing up against her backside.

Dating Calhoun had been all about the sex. Going out had been almost an afterthought. By the time they were adults their teenage patterns had already been established.

The elevator doors slid open. Bruce looked just as surprised to see them as they were to see him. He'd been headed toward the bridge, not the elevator, but turned toward it now. Dan recovered more quickly. He held the button to shut the door. Then pushed another for the top floor.

Knowing what it must look like to Calhoun, Mitzi held her breath all the way up. "Dan?"

"I just want one night of kissing you without a basketball to the head. Maybe he'll finally get the message."

Mitzi choked back a laugh. They kissed, riding the elevator several more times before Dan took her home and kissed her breathless at her door. The coach got his wish.

No basketball tonight.

THOUGH HE PRETENDED not to be, her dad had been waiting up for her. He set a hot cocoa down in front of her, like the ones her mom used to make, with tiny marshmallows. Then he joined her at the kitchen table.

"Did you have a nice night?"

"Uh-hmm." She blew on the steam rising from the cup. He always made it too hot. When she saw his concerned gaze across the table, she found it hard to hold back the tears. But she managed with a smile.

"I'm okay," she said. "It's just hot chocolate and holidays making me crazy." Sighing into her cup, she set it back down. "Lights downtown…this being mom's favorite time of year." She rubbed the back of her neck. "Bruce being back. And missing Freddie so much."

"It's not fair, is it? First your mother, then your brother." He reached across the table to pat her hand. "You can always come back to the support group."

She shook her head. There was only one person she wanted to talk to about Freddie. "Dan kissed me tonight," she said, as if those two thoughts were somehow connected. "We've kissed before, but…" This was different. "It's starting to feel like I have a future again."

"Honey," he said, "that's a good thing."

Except… Kissing Dan… Dancing with Bruce.

It was all so confusing. She didn't know how to let go of her past. Let him go? He was leaving.

"Do you think Bruce and I could ever be friends again?"

"Of course you can, if that's something you both want."

"You don't understand, Dad. I did the one thing Bruce will never forgive me for. I contracted Keith Calhoun for the Navy yesterday."

THE HOUSE WAS QUIET when he got home. He'd taken the light rail and spent the past several hours riding to the end of the line and back.

He kept flashing to that elevator.

He didn't bother turning on his bedroom light but went straight to the window facing hers. Her room was dark. Like the rest of her dad's house. Bruce leaned against the window frame as he unbuttoned his jacket.

He got to hold her on the dance floor. He couldn't ask for much more than that. For the past eighteen months he'd had the single-minded goal of returning to his unit. He'd refused to touch her, rebuffed her attempts to comfort him. And denied them both that emotional and physical release.

Because he knew he'd be leaving as soon as he was able. He'd seen firsthand what losing Freddie had done to her. How could he put her through that again if, God forbid, something *else* should happen to him?

In an attempt to do what was best for her, he'd forgotten that he simply wasn't complete without her. As selfish as it seemed, there wasn't anything he wouldn't give, including his good leg, to touch her one last time.

A white comforter streaming across the Zahns' snow-covered backyard toward the trampoline caught his attention. "What the hell is she doing?"

Wasn't she spending the night at the hotel?

Bruce scrambled downstairs and out the back door, then hopped the chain-link fence between the two yards. The trampoline, where he and Freddie used to build forts in the summer, had a safety net as a precaution against their roughhousing.

Unzipping the enclosure, he found Mitzi bundled in the comforter, staring up at the night sky. The posted No Shoes sign had faded, but he still kicked off his dress shoes to climb up onto the trampoline with her.

"What do you think you're doing, Chief?"

"Stargazing."

The tracks of her tears told a different story.

"It's November," he said, crawling under the covers with her. "You're in your party dress and bare feet."

"I have my overcoat on and a blanket. I'll go back inside when I get cold," she said in a small voice.

She was already cold enough to be shivering.

"Not if you fall asleep and freeze to death." The snow-dusted tarp beneath them was already frozen, with cold air circulating from underneath. At least the snowfall had stopped sometime earlier in the evening. "Come here," he said, spooning her for body heat.

He held her while her shivering subsided. Then he continued to hold her as she relaxed, snuggling her round bottom against a part of him that wanted more than snuggling.

He kept his body in check by humming the "Marines' Hymn" in her ear.

"If you don't stop I'll start singing 'From the halls of Montezuma…'"

But her threat was an empty one. She picked up the last few lines and sang them to him. "If the Army and the Navy ever gaze on heaven's scenes, they will find the streets are guarded by United States Marines."

"That's a promise," he said, brushing the soft curls back so he could see her face. So he could commit it to memory. As if it wasn't etched there already.

"I miss him," she said after a while.

Bruce filled his lungs with frigid night air. "I know." He exhaled.

"What do you remember?"

Enough that he didn't want to talk about it. She didn't have to clarify what she was asking. He knew.

"Don't think," she said, shifting onto her back until she was looking up at him. "Just tell me your first thoughts after the grenade hit your convoy."

"You don't want to know," he answered.

"I thanked God you were alive," she said.

It warmed him inside and out to hear it from her lips.

"That was my second thought," he admitted.

"Did it hurt?"

He shook his head. Shock had kept him from feeling much of anything at first. "He didn't feel it coming," he said, answering the question behind her question.

"I can't believe he's gone."

He knew exactly how she felt.

"I'm sorry, Mitz. I should have done a better job of watching out for him, for you." It was the first time he'd voiced the burden of responsibility he carried for Freddie's death.

How could he ask her forgiveness when he

couldn't forgive himself? But he wanted it so badly.

"It wasn't your fault, Calhoun," she said, giving it unconditionally.

"You don't know that."

"I know you," she said. "Do you want to know my second thought after I thanked God you were alive?"

Of course he did.

"How fast I could get to your bedside."

Her gaze dropped to his mouth.

Which suddenly felt dry.

That would have been quite a come-on if her weepy eyes hadn't been telling him sex was the furthest thing from her mind. "A kiss is such a silly thing to cry about, don't you think?" she asked.

He agreed. "No crying, Chief." He wiped away her free-falling tears. "Tears freeze."

She choked back a laugh. At least she was laughing.

"Promise me I won't lose you, too?" In that moment he would have promised her anything. But what he should have done was kiss her to keep those next words from passing her lips. "That no matter what happens, Calhoun, we will always be friends."

Friends? Why did she think he kept pushing her away? He couldn't be friends. He couldn't be near her without wanting her.

He took her hand that brushed his cheek—her left hand—and planted a kiss where his ring would have been, had she still loved him. Had he allowed himself to love her. She fell asleep in his arms without realizing he never made that promise.

When the snow started to fall again, he carried her inside.

CHAPTER ELEVEN

IT TOOK MITZI THREE DAYS in bed to get over her cold and a week to catch up on the two days of work she'd missed. Dan had sent her a bouquet of flowers and a balloon with get-well wishes. She was looking forward to their ski weekend in Vail.

Bruce had a crate of oranges delivered to her door.

Since her return to work he'd kept a professional, polite distance. And every day since she'd drawn up the enlistment papers for Keith Calhoun was another day spent waiting for the proverbial other boot to drop.

True to her word, Mitzi hadn't said anything to any member of the Calhoun family about Heather's pregnancy or Keith's enlistment. Keith was of legal age and he would have to find the courage to tell them himself.

Her biggest fear was that he wouldn't find the courage before Bruce found out. Either way, she was the bad guy. Not just because she'd enlisted his brother, but because she didn't confide in him. On paper it looked even worse because she needed Keith in her last-quarter stats to meet her recruiting quota.

That's not why she'd done it, though. And Keith's threats to join the Army, while upsetting to Bruce, had little to no effect on her. Not even Heather's pregnancy had been a factor. She hoped Keith and Heather *didn't* get married. At least not so young. And not just for the sake of the baby.

Keith had won her over with his paper on Iwo Jima. And she saw what Bruce didn't—a Marine. Not just a Marine—a Navy Corpsman who served with the Corps. The guy everyone called Doc.

The guy who ran toward you when you fell. The guy who covered you with his own body while you were down. And the guy who picked up a gun if he had to.

That's why she'd been willing to open that back door into the Marine Corps for him and enlist Keith in the Navy. Not that Bruce would understand.

Aside from Keith Calhoun, Mitzi had several prospective recruits in various stages of enlistment to keep her busy through the holidays to the end of the year.

Things started to settle down that Wednesday afternoon the week of Thanksgiving. She hoped to leave early enough for a quick trip to the grocery store before going home. Otherwise she'd get caught up in the crowd of last-minute turkey shoppers.

Around three o'clock, she'd just finished with her last appointment of the day when Angela walked in. The young single mom nodded to Mitzi, but went straight to Calhoun's desk and handed him what must have been a marriage license.

Angela appeared none the worse for her venture. And no one was more surprised about that than Mitzi. "So you met Hatch?" Mitzi asked when Calhoun excused himself to photocopy Angela's documents.

"Yes."

"How was he?"

"Fine," she said, sticking to one-word answers that did nothing to satisfy Mitzi's curiosity.

Hatch had been a Navy SEAL before he'd lost an eye and his peripheral vision. Which meant he could no longer do the job he'd trained for and loved. That more than losing his eye was what had made him bitter. But it was his burn scars most people couldn't get past.

"You're offside, Chief," Bruce warned.

Behind enemy lines.

If he only knew how right he was.

She gave Calhoun a measured look, which he ignored.

To Angela he said, "The Navy's still open to you, Angela. If you'd rather—"

"No." She cut him off with a shake of her head. "I'm here to join the Marines."

Calhoun shrugged in apology to Mitzi. That he'd even offered Angela a choice was nice, but not necessary. She was his recruit. He'd put in the extra effort. And he'd earned her loyalty.

"So tell me what your interests are and we'll see what kind of jobs the Marine Corps has to offer you...." He finished up a half hour later with "Are you looking to leave before Christmas?" Boot camp was thirteen weeks in Parris Island, South Carolina.

"Oh, wow," Angela said, "I hadn't even thought about that." Clearly she was worried about her young son over the holidays.

"After Christmas," Calhoun said.

Angela stood to go as Keith Calhoun walked in, followed by Lucky Calhoun carrying his son, Chance, bundled up against the cooler weather. Keith held the door for Angela as she passed the brothers on her way out.

Mitzi braced herself for the inevitable confrontation with Bruce.

She'd become accustomed to seeing Keith after school as he continued to work out with the other DEPers. But she'd canceled her DEP classes and physical training for the rest of the week because of Thanksgiving.

As far as she knew, Lucky Calhoun had never

stopped by just for a visit. Mitzi stood. She didn't want to be sitting behind her desk for this.

"Favor to ask," Lucky said to both her and Bruce.

"What's that?" Bruce asked.

Don't hate me forever.

"Can I make your office an official drop-off location for the Corps' Toys for Tots campaign? Seems I volunteered to chair our local chapter this year."

She was so relieved, she answered for both of them. "Absolutely." Not that Bruce would object to collecting new toys for less fortunate youngsters at Christmas.

"You have that big empty loft upstairs, right?" Lucky asked. "I could really use the free storage."

"It's yours," Mitzi said. The upstairs loft had been a ballet studio at one time. It had as much square footage as both recruiting offices, plus outside access via fire stairs. Or inside via the back hall stairs that ran between both offices.

"Thank you, Mitzi," Lucky said.

"You might want to ask my dad about barrels, too."

"Already done," he said. "Cait baked a couple extra pies for tomorrow at the bowling alley, too."

"Do you want me to pick them up?" she offered. By keeping Lucky engaged in rather benign conversation there was no chance for confrontation.

"We'll deliver," Lucky said. "Bruce, wanna help me unload the barrels? Here." He handed Chance to Keith. "Watch your nephew."

Bruce slapped his hat on his head and Lucky and Bruce headed outside.

Keith looked terrified.

And much too young to be an expectant father.

"May I?" Mitzi asked, taking the toddler from him.

LUCKY RAISED THE DOOR of the rental truck. Bruce reached in and grabbed two empty barrels. This wasn't a two-man chore, so he knew something was up. "You couldn't get Keith to do this for you?"

"I could have," Lucky said, "but that's what I wanted to talk to you about. Keith's under enough pressure without you adding to it."

"What on earth does a high school kid know about stress and pressure?"

"Why don't you ask him?"

"Is Keith in some kind of trouble?"

Lucky remained silent.

"Drugs?" That didn't sound like Keith. "Girl trouble?"

There was a barely perceptible tightening around his brother's mouth.

"How deep?"

"'Bout as deep as you can get."

Bruce cursed under his breath. "He's not joining up to run away, is he?"

"I don't think so."

"Said the man who enlisted in the Corps at seventeen. If I recall, you needed Uncle John to sign off on that enlistment."

"Keith's eighteen. He doesn't need anyone's permission."

"Am I the only one who cares that the kid is intent on blowing off college?"

"Bruce," Lucky said, "if he wants to go to college, he'll go to college. If he doesn't, he won't. It's his life."

"The Marine Corps will still be here four years from now—after he graduates college."

"Yeah, but will Keith? From what I hear it may already be too late." Lucky shot a glance toward the recruiting offices.

Bruce followed his gaze. The Army/Air Force side was already dark. He knew for a fact Mike was out of town all week, back east with his girlfriend and her family.

Lucky slapped Bruce on the shoulder. "What are your teens and twenties for if not to make a few mistakes? I made my share. Now I'm running Big Luke's motorcycle dealership. Designing my own custom bikes. Married to Cait. I have a healthy, happy son. Another on the way. Did you ever think I'd settle down and become a weekend warrior?"

Bruce sat on the bumper next to his brother. Crossing his arms, he stretched his feet out in front of him. "Ever feel guilty?"

"Why, because I married Little Luke's widow?"

"If Luke hadn't died, would you be this happy?"

"My life would be different, that's for sure. But Cait and I try not to look at it that way. Her having loved her first husband doesn't take anything away from our marriage. And our love for each other doesn't dishonor Luke's memory in any way."

"Sometimes I feel like I don't deserve to be happy."

"Why would you say that?"

"I screwed up."

"We all screw up."

"Yeah, but I hurt the people I care about most."

"Live a good life, Bruce. That's how we honor those who served and went before us."

"I THOUGHT YOU DIDN'T want kids," Calhoun said, taking down one of the bar aprons from a hook on the wall and tying it around his trim waist. It wasn't often that she got to see him out of uniform, but today he was dressed casually in a navy-blue-and-white pinstripe button-down shirt and jeans.

Mitzi had him peeling potatoes in the bar's small but well-appointed stainless steel kitchen. He'd showed up on her doorstep at 0600 sharp to help cart everything that wasn't already there over in the Hummer.

And he hadn't let up on the subject of kids since he'd seen her holding his nephew Chance yesterday. It was her own fault, really. For Keith's sake, she'd been trying to get Bruce used to the idea that he'd have a niece or another nephew soon.

"I never said I didn't want kids."

"I'm pretty sure you did," he said. "At least not with me." He didn't sound angry or bitter. Just matter-of-fact. But that wasn't the way she remembered their one and only conversation about kids.

"I thought we'd decided together that it was difficult enough for us to find time together. And that a family wouldn't be in anyone's best interest."

This subject was becoming painful.

What did it matter now?

They were at different work stations with their backs to each other and Mitzi stopped chopping celery to turn and look at him. "I want kids," she admitted.

He stopped peeling. "Does Estrada? Do you see yourself having kids with him, I mean?"

"I don't know," she said, leaning back against

the counter and stuffing her hands into the angled pockets of her apron. "We're not there yet."

She had on a frilly black-and-white apron in a paisley print with striped accents that was fancier and more feminine than the plain white V-neck and jeans she wore with a comfortable pair of flats. "I can't see myself having kids." He went back to peeling potatoes. "Not yet, anyway."

She started chopping again. "Yeah, well, that's why they invented birth control." She was glad his back was to her so he couldn't see the emotions that played across her face.

"Ouch!" When she glanced over her shoulder, he was sucking on his finger.

She crossed to his work station near the sink and ran the cold water. "I was wondering how long until you peeled your finger."

"It's just a nick."

"Stick it under the faucet and I'll get a Band-Aid," she said, heading to the wall-mounted first aid kit.

"It's nothing."

"Let me see." She turned off the water. His finger was still bleeding. *Nothing, my ass.* But it wasn't deep. She applied pressure with a clean dish towel.

They stood facing each other in awkward silence while she held his finger. After peeking at his still-bleeding finger, she replaced the towel and reapplied pressure.

"Freddie put the idea in my head," he confessed. "That doesn't make it a bad idea. He wanted to be an uncle, did you know that?"

She felt as if her heart would leap out of her chest. But just because Freddie and Bruce had discussed kids didn't mean she should get all tangled up in the idea. "I didn't know that," she confessed.

He brushed the hair from her eyes with his free hand. "I liked what we had," he said, tilting her chin. She could hear the desire in his voice and felt herself responding to it. She'd never stopped wanting him. But now she also had feelings for Dan. This was so complicated. How could she be attracted to two men at the same time?

Besides, Bruce wouldn't want her once he knew she'd enlisted his brother against his express wishes.

"Bleeding's stopped," she said as casually as she could. She let go of Calhoun's finger and handed him the Band-Aid and antibiotic ointment.

"Hi," Dan said, walking into the kitchen. *Thank God,* she thought. "Brought my apron." He held up a BBQ apron that read: Kiss the Cook. "Where do you want me?"

She smiled at his innuendo as he wrapped his arms around her and gave her a kiss. He seemed to angle them slightly...toward Bruce? She must be imagining that.

"Bruce could use some help peeling potatoes." She handed him a second peeler and gave him a small shove. "Not counting family and friends, we usually get around fifty drop-in guests, give or take." She lifted two more ten-pound bags from the rack under the sink to the counter.

"I suppose you want kids," Bruce said to Dan. Mitzi abruptly turned and glared at Calhoun.

"Yeah," Dan admitted, looking between her and Bruce.

"How many?" Bruce asked.

"Well, not fifty," Dan said, eyeing them.

Mitzi was still laughing when she went to check on the turkeys. The large commercial rotisserie meant they could roast half a dozen at a time and kept the double oven free for heating side dishes and pies.

Her dad had been cooking around the clock, starting the day before. Another half dozen roasted turkeys were in the walk-in refrigerator, waiting to be reheated just before they were served.

They went by the pound-per-person rule. Slightly smaller birds fit in the rotisserie better, cooked faster and ensured they had enough drumsticks to go around.

Her dad had been doing this for several years now—he had his routine down pat. He'd gone

home for a shower and a change and a quick nap
when she and Bruce had arrived shortly after six
o'clock.

He was back now, along with Nora Jean and
Audrey and a couple of the bowling alley's other
employees. Mitzi left Audrey in charge of the stuffing and showed Nora Jean where the linens were
kept, then left her to organize tablecloths and cen-
terpieces. They used paper plates, paper napkins
and plastic wear for convenience, but she liked to
make it look nice.

There were a number of tables in the bar, and
the built-in tables behind each lane. Bruce and
Dan finished peeling potatoes much faster than
she'd expected—highly competitive as they both
were—and while she set the pots to boil the two
were setting up folding tables and folding chairs
running the length of the bowling alley. Did they
have to turn *that* into a race, too?

The two pool tables would be covered with plywood and draped with tablecloths and the buffet
set up there.

When Lucky and Cait dropped in with pies,
Bruce stopped racing Dan to bounce his nephew
on his knee. But he kept one eye on the other man's
progress, Mitzi noticed.

It was afternoon before Mitzi knew it.

Henry arrived early. As with most of their
guests, he preferred to come into the bowling

alley through the back alley door. Her father kept it propped open, inviting in anyone who happened to wander by.

"This is my favorite day of the year," Henry commented as he rolled by her with a loaded plate in his lap.

THIS HAD TO BE his least favorite day of the year, Bruce decided. No, that wasn't true.

He was just exhausted. He'd stayed for cleanup.

But so had Dan.

Mitzi had walked the schoolteacher to his car ten minutes ago and she still wasn't back. Bruce tied off the garbage bag with an extra *oomph* to the knot. He picked up the three others he'd tied and headed to the Dumpster.

It turned out Dan had parked out back.

But then, Bruce knew that.

It was dark, just after six o'clock. Dan was parked in the shadows, leaning against his dark SUV. Bruce could see by the couple's silhouette that they weren't touching, but they were awfully close to touching.

Mitzi's laughter carried to him.

Bruce's mouth held a grim line.

"You just gonna stand there while he kisses her?" Henry rolled from behind the Dumpster to where Bruce could see him. "Make some noise."

"What are you doing out here, old man?" Bruce tossed the garbage bags, unnoticed by the couple.

"I'm not some damn voyeur, if that's what you're thinking."

"You can't be scrounging. You had plenty to eat."

"Sometimes I scrounge for information…and other things," he said.

Fred stepped into the alley and tossed a couple more garbage bags into the Dumpster, heedless of the noise he made.

Mitzi and Dan looked up. And between one heartbeat and the next Bruce had figured out what he wanted to give Mitzi for Christmas.

CHAPTER TWELVE

FOLLOWING THIS WEEKEND, Bruce might never be ready for kids, after all. He had six of them and their gear loaded into his USMC Hummer. Heather sat in the passenger seat beside him, making him nervous the way she looked him over.

His brother, the boys he thought of as the SEAL twins, the corpsman recruit and the gamer were all piled into the backseat. Keith, as per usual, was texting. The other boys were, as his mother would say, roughhousing.

As long as they were all buckled in and he had the signed permission slips of those who weren't quite eighteen, he didn't care that they were getting a little rowdy back there.

Vail was about a hundred miles west of Denver up I-70. It had taken them two hours to get to town and they still had a ways to go to get to the cabin. Bruce couldn't blame them for being excited. He was excited.

But he had more than just Heather to be nervous

about. He hadn't skied in years and he was about to go skiing for the first time with a prosthesis.

He was bringing up the rear of their little caravan. Dan was out front in his Ford Bronco with another six kids. He was followed by Mitzi in her dad's van—because it was bigger than her CR-V—and Annie in her Subaru, a good snow car. The women had four kids each.

He shared joint responsibility for twenty teenagers. Yeah, having any of his own was the last thing on his mind at the moment.

MITZI LOOKED in the rearview mirror. The three girls in the backseat of her dad's van had plugged in to the latest Zac Efron movie. Kelly sat beside her in the front.

She was texting someone and kept looking over at Mitzi as if she had something she wanted to say. "Mitzi?" she finally asked.

"Hmm?"

Kelly glanced over her shoulder at the other girls before continuing. "I don't think I'm going to go into the Navy."

"Why not?"

Please do not let this be because Keith joined. Kelly would be giving up the opportunity of a lifetime because of a boy.

Kelly shrugged. "I'm going to visit my grandma in Arizona at Christmas. And I might decide to stay. So I might not even finish out my senior year at Englewood. I could just test out and get my GED and not even go back to school. That's what I'm thinking, anyway."

"Kelly," Mitzi said, "it doesn't matter where you decide to live. Please just promise me you'll get your high school diploma."

She was too smart and too talented to quit. But Mitzi noticed the drummer girl never made her that promise.

BRUCE PULLED IN behind Dan and set his parking brake.

It took some maneuvering to get all four vehicles parked behind the cabin. The three-car garage was on a level beneath the house.

Dan offered the women the use of the garage for their smaller cars. The third bay was taken up by a couple of snowmobiles. But the Bronco and Hummer wouldn't have fit anyway.

The cabin was older, well maintained, with rustic wood siding and shingles. Dan had either inherited it, had connections or money. Maybe all three.

This was not the kind of cabin a guy could afford on a schoolteacher's salary—or a soldier's either. And it wasn't the kind of cabin that went on the market very often. When it did, it went to someone who could afford a couple million for a vacation home.

Access to the cabin was a steep rock climb over wide, snow-covered stone steps. Again Bruce brought up the rear as all twenty teens raced ahead of the adults.

He didn't want any witnesses in case he slipped and fell.

MITZI SLOWED HER STEPS so Bruce could catch up. He didn't appear to be having any problems with the climb. The pace he set was more deliberate.

Dan led them past the front door, around a stone path running along the side of the cabin to the back. Here they had ski racks to dump their snowboards, skis, poles and boots. The covered hot tub elicited a few giggles from the teens. And Annie.

Luckily Dan had supplied the chaperones with the same printed packing list he'd given the kids, so Mitzi had remembered to bring her tankini and beach towel.

Mitzi smiled at him as the group unloaded their equipment into the racks and the excited chorus of "Mr. Estrada, Mr. Estrada, when can we go skiing?"

Skiing was an expensive sport and Dan had paid for Kelly and a couple others who didn't have the money for equipment rental and lift tickets. Mitzi thought the world of him for that. "Have I thanked you yet, *Mr. Estrada?*"

"We just got here," he said.

"Then thank you for inviting me."

He wrapped his arm around her waist for a squeeze. "You're welcome," he said into her ear.

Dan gave her a quick kiss, then unlocked the French doors. "Stomp off your boots outside," he reminded everyone as he turned on the lights and adjusted the thermostat.

"Nice place you got here, Bubba," Annie said with her eyes toward the vaulted ceilings.

There was a half loft with two bedrooms upstairs and two downstairs and a bathroom on each floor. Now, that was going to be a problem among twenty-four guests, almost half of them teenage girls.

"Absolutely beautiful, Dan," Mitzi said, admiring the wood paneling and the stone fireplace taking up an entire wall at one end of the open living area.

Bruce, who was bringing up the rear, stomped off outside and followed the last of the kids in, making sure the door was closed behind them.

The girls were to divvy up the bedrooms how they saw fit and the guys were going to be camped out in the living room.

Dan turned to Bruce. "There's a queen-size bed

in one of the downstairs rooms if you'd be more comfortable."

"Thank you, no," Bruce declined—as Mitzi knew he would. "Floor's fine."

"Plenty of Army cots and wool blankets if you need one, Marine. Just let me know."

Dan was just being a polite host, but Bruce scoffed as if insulted at being offered a cot. Specifically an Army cot. Oblivious to the undercurrent between the men, the young males dumped their sleeping bags in a corner by the fireplace. Dan and Bruce handed them their car keys and the boys raced back down the hill to bring up their food supplies, most of which had been packed into the Hummer and the Bronco.

Enough to feed a small army of teens.

Again thanks to Dan.

Mitzi and Annie took an upstairs room with a couple of twin beds. This left another room with twin beds, a room with two sets of bunk beds and the room with a queen-size bed—seven beds for ten girls.

"There are plenty of beds to go around," Dan reassured them as he directed the staging of the good old Army cots. By the time the girls, who'd also brought their sleeping bags, had their sleeping arrangements figured out, the boys had returned with the supplies.

Bruce supervised the storage, with everyone

eager to help. The sooner things got put away, the sooner they'd be on the slopes.

"All right, then," Dan said, rubbing his hands together. "Who's ready for their first run of the day?"

"I am!" Mitzi chimed in with the eager chorus.

Dan held her back as everyone scrambled out the door. "I wanted to ask you something," he said. "And I'm too excited to wait."

"Okay," she said, responding to the glint in his eye. Her back was to the wall and they were standing near the open French doors.

"Do you think—" he started playing with a strand of her hair "—we could come back here over Christmas break? Just the two of us?"

Calhoun cleared his throat. "Forgot my gloves," he said, pointing toward the kitchen. "Won't take me but a minute."

Mitzi straightened and Dan put his hands in his pockets, waiting for Bruce to retrieve his gloves and leave.

"As you were," Calhoun ordered on his way out the door, as if they were a couple of raw recruits in his charge.

WHILE EVERYONE ELSE MADE their way over to the resort Bruce decided to stick to the private run, which was little more than a beginner slope with a rope tow.

He'd read about a Marine, an above-the-knee amputee, who'd returned to extreme skiing in just one day on the slopes. He was determined to do as well or better.

He'd waited until everyone was out of the house, including Mitzi and Dan, before changing out his snow boots for ski boots and skis. In his ski socks Bruce sat on one of the many benches built into the deck outside the cabin. He opened the tongue wide on both boots. Reached for his left boot before grabbing the right. He put his right ski on first, because that was easiest.

But funny how a lifetime of putting on his left shoe first had become ingrained. He stood and stomped down on the heel to seat the boot, then sat back down and buckled it until it was snug, but not tight.

He repeated the same procedure on his left. Only, when he stomped down he had to use his best judgment to determine if he'd seated the boot. And a snug fit didn't matter as much as getting his boot on his prosthetic foot nice and tight. He bent forward at the knees a couple of times to make sure his heels were in the heel box.

He was good to go.

Cautiously at first, he made his way across the deck in the clunky boots and down the steps, across the snow-covered yard toward the rack with his skis. The backyard here was fairly level.

He laid down his skis, picked up his poles and cleared the snow from his left boot first this time. For stability he'd decided to put his right ski on last. He slid the lip of his left boot under the lip of the left binding. Lining the heel of the boot up with the back binding, he dropped the heel into the heel cup and pushed down until it clicked. Then repeated the process on his right side.

He bent at the knee a couple of times. So far so good. Now all he had to do was snowplow his way down the slight slope to the right and he'd be on that private run. Keeping his skis in the V was the easiest way to start because two skis in a straight line wanted to travel at different speeds.

The snowplow wasn't used by someone who could ski well. He practiced a couple of snowplow runs, then added some snowplow turns. The ski with the most weight had the most control, so more often than not he turned to his left, the ski with less control.

The cabin's private run connected to one of Vail's many trails. So they still needed lift tickets to enjoy the resort. He could see Dan, Mitzi, Annie and several of the kids already hitting the powder with season passes on their ski jackets.

The rest, like Bruce, had purchased a weekend

pass just before the trip. His skis were old and had sat in the garage for several winters unused.

He'd borrowed the jacket and pants from his brother. According to their mother, his old gear had somehow ended up at Goodwill. That's what he got for not coming home more than once every couple of years.

But it felt pretty darn good to be on skis again. He might not be ready for carving or jumping, but after a few hours he was ready to take it to the slopes. Just to be on the safe side he practiced falling down and getting up a couple times first.

As long as he remembered to keep his skis sideways to the slope, and that getting up on his right was easier than getting up on his left, he would do.

By the end of the day he'd worked his way up from beginner to intermediate slopes. And had advanced from snowplow turns to parallel turns and hockey stops. He couldn't wait until tomorrow to carve out another slope.

He wasn't the first one to call it a day. When he got back to the cabin Keith and Heather were already there in their pj's. They looked awfully guilty when he came in.

Bruce narrowed his eyes.

"What?" Keith asked.

"Show a little respect. And restraint."

MITZI SKIED RIGHT UP to the last run of the day. She'd done a pretty good job of keeping up with Dan only because he'd come down to her level.

She felt most comfortable on the intermediate slopes, but had tried a couple expert runs with his encouragement.

Dan's ability went beyond expert. He was a trained, all-terrain soldier. He'd fought in the mountains of Afghanistan in the snow and bitter cold.

As they were putting away their skis for the night, she found herself alone with Dan for a few minutes. Not one to pass up the opportunity, he hugged her close—as close as their ski jackets allowed—and traced her face with his cold fingers, quietly giving her a little history about his former unit, the famed 10th Mountain Division. "Vail was started by a handful of veterans of the 10th," he whispered. Kissing her chin, he added slowly, "They trained at Camp Hale, Colorado, during World War Two and returned afterward to become instructors. Then—" he kissed her gently on the lips "—they realized their dream by founding this resort."

They stood staring at each other for what seemed like an eternity. Mitzi had no idea how she felt about this kind, generous man. He'd even arranged to treat them to a demonstration by the 10th Mountain (Light). Disentangling herself from his arms, she said, "It's a shame Mike couldn't come. He'd probably have all these boys, and some of the girls, signing up for the Army." Dan laughed and steered her toward the cabin.

But if Mike had come, Bruce wouldn't be here.

Bruce.

She wondered where he'd been all day. She hadn't seen him on any of her runs.

When they walked in through the French doors, Bruce and Annie were in the kitchen. Annie stood holding a three-pound spaghetti package in each hand. "Help, do you know how to cook for twenty starving teens?"

"As a matter of fact, I do," Mitzi said. "Let me just go get changed."

MITZI WAS A GOOD COOK. From the look in Estrada's eye the man still had an appetite for dessert, Bruce thought. A couple of the girls got out the ingredients for s'mores. While Estrada built the fire, Bruce supervised the s'more making and after-dinner cleanup.

"Mr. Estrada?" one of the girls asked. "Can we get in the hot tub now?"

"Only eight at a time," he said.

Several of the girls ran off to put on their bathing suits, leaving Bruce alone in the kitchen with Heather. Annie stepped in to help with the s'mores. "Heather, go put a bra on," Annie said, snapping a graham cracker in half. The girl turned beet-red and disappeared. "You didn't notice that?" she asked him.

"I did," he said, "but unlike you, I wasn't going to say anything in front of everyone." Besides, that would be admitting he noticed.

"It's probably best you didn't react," Annie said, ignoring his reprimand. "That girl's been trying to get your attention all evening."

Bruce wasn't so sure Heather was trying to get his attention as much as she was trying to get Keith's by making him jealous.

Bruce glanced over at Mitzi toasting marsh-mallows.

"You gonna get in the hot tub tonight for the adult swim, Calhoun?" Annie asked, nibbling chocolate and looking up at him.

"I didn't bring my suit."

"Neither did I." She winked at him, then left him alone in the kitchen to think about that.

Chaperones in need of chaperones.

How screwed up was that?

DAN HAD DIMMED THE LIGHTS and put a movie in the DVD player. The kids who weren't in and out of the hot tub had their sleeping bags spread out on the floor in front of the big-screen TV, watching one of the stupidest movies Mitzi had ever seen, about hot-tub time travel.

It was after eleven before most of the kids had settled for the night. Mitzi stood and stretched.

"Are you going to put your swimsuit on?" Dan asked.

Actually, she'd been going to put her pj's on to go to bed. But she wouldn't mind trying the hot tub.

And she had that brand-new tankini she'd got on clearance a few months ago. "I thought I might," she said.

"Mind if I join you?"

BRUCE WAS IN THE BATHROOM wringing out his brother's wet swim trunks. He'd ducked in right after he saw Dan coming out with his trunks on. He'd be damned if he was going to let Dan be out there alone with Mitzi.

He'd been invited along to chaperone a bunch of horny teenagers—well, not invited, volunteered. But he was here to chaperone. And he didn't care if that horny *teenager* was eighteen or twenty-eight.

"Shit!" Keith's wet trunks were cold. He wrapped the equally wet beach towel around his waist, wishing he'd had the time to run both through the dryer. He stepped into his brother's flip-flops. His junk was going to shrivel up like an old man the minute he hit that thirty-two-degree air outside.

Estrada was the only one in the tub.

The lights were low. The music was slow.

Oldest trick in the book. Get there first and set the mood. If Estrada's trunks were gone there were going to be fists-a-flying.

But Estrada, lucky him, had his trunks on underneath those bubbles. He just didn't look happy to see Bruce.

The jets were bubbling and steam was rising. Nothing like getting into a hot tub when the air outside was cold enough that you could see your breath in front of your face.

If Bruce had been here to relax he might have taken his leg off and really enjoyed it. As it was he decided he might want to keep his leg on.

Guess he'd find out just how good those modifications were that made his C-Leg a swim leg.

"You can get that wet?" Estrada asked.

"Whole lot of advances in prosthetics," he said, climbing the stairs to the tub. He stepped in left foot first and sat across from Estrada. They were staring each other down when Mitzi came out.

Shivering, she dropped her towel over a chair and tiptoed up the stairs. She was wearing a pink-floral-on-black two-piece with just a hint of skin showing between the pink top and the black bottom.

"This is heaven," she said, moving to the opposite side of the tub and sitting between them.

Annie must have found a swimsuit. She came

out in a fluffy pink bathrobe, which she dropped at the top of the stairs. Okay, no swimsuit. But she had on a tank top and a pink thong. Air Force Annie, the blonde bombshell, was a double D, and that tank top was going to look mighty interesting wet.

MITZI WAS A RESPECTABLE B cup. Men did not drool over her breasts. But she liked to think her breasts were proportionate to her size. Annie was not a respectable B cup and she'd been sticking to Bruce like glue all day—ever since the hot tub foursome last night—and Mitzi didn't like it one bit.

The thing was she had no right to be jealous.

Mitzi had already decided she and Calhoun made better friends than lovers. And since his return, she really hadn't given Dan a chance.

She and Dan were carving out a slope together, wind whipping at her cheeks. Dan was tearing up the moguls while she was doing her best to keep up.

When they reached the bottom of the hill, she stopped and raised her goggles. "I never did answer your question."

"And...?" he prompted.

"I'd like to come back at Christmas," she said.

He caught on really quickly. He leaned over his skis to kiss her.

She kissed him back with a thoroughness she'd

never allowed herself before. He tasted of spearmint.

"If there weren't twenty-two other people staying with us right now—" He growled deep in his throat, letting her know exactly how much he wanted to reach that next level.

And those twenty-two other people were never far behind. "Whoa, Mr. Estrada," one kid said, sliding past.

"Break it up, you two," Annie teased, spraying them with powder as she turned into a stop.

Mitzi wiped away the zinc lip balm she'd left on Dan's cheek. When she looked up, Calhoun was there, watching them. He took a pack of cinnamon gum from his pocket. "Gum, anyone?"

THE 10TH MOUNTAIN (Light) Division arrived in style the next day. Their group watched the demonstration in shock and awe from the top of the basin as the mountain men jumped out of a helicopter with their skis on, into the back bowls, and worked their way down.

A second lieutenant with the 10th met their group on the mountain and provided the commentary as his men skied. They used the private trail at the back of the cabin for a more hands-on demonstration, showcasing their equipment. And for a shooting demonstration, proving just how accurate they were whether on snowmobiles or skis.

Afterward the entire group agreed they wanted one last run before heading home. The adults, including some of Dan's buddies, had taken the Skyline Express lift and were standing at the top of Blue Sky Basin.

Everything to the left of the lift was steep and fast. Double black diamonds, X-treme double black diamonds and unmarked terrain with trails that were mere suggestions of trails.

Mitzi knew she was going right. Annie and a couple of her new admirers from the 10th also headed in that direction.

Clearly, Dan wanted to go left with his buddies. "If it's all right with you."

"Go," she said with a parting kiss. She'd been holding him back all weekend.

Besides, it wasn't Dan she was worried about. Bruce looked as if he had every intention of following the extreme team.

But he wasn't ready for this.

"Where do you think you're going?" she asked.

"Down a mountain."

"You—"

"Shh. Don't say *can't* right now, Chief. It would spoil the moment. You could just send me on my way with a kiss, like you did him."

"Calhoun, you coming or not?" Dan called back.

Bruce glanced over his shoulder, then back

at her. "Or you could beg me to stay with your kisses."

"Don't be stupid, Bruce," she said as he turned away toward the ridge.

Mitzi hesitated a moment. That man was going to get himself killed.

She caught up to Annie on the way down.

By the time they reached the bottom, it was clear by the number of ski patrol snowmobiles there was something going on up the mountain.

Her stomach knotted when she saw Keith and her Navy SEAL recruits racing toward her.

"Oh, man!" Keith came to a hockey stop beside them. "He broke his freakin' leg."

"I'm going to kill him!" Mitzi didn't know whether to be angry or thankful that it was his leg and not his neck. "I knew your brother was going to get himself hurt."

"Not Bruce," Keith said. "Mr. Estrada."

CHAPTER THIRTEEN

CALHOUN TOOK CHARGE of shuffling cars and kids, since Dan, with his thigh-high cast, could no longer drive down the mountain. Annie drove Dan's Bronco, while Keith drove Annie's Subaru. Annie and Bruce both took on extra passengers so that Keith and Mitzi could ride with one less.

Keith because of his inexperience. And Mitzi so that Dan could relax. Although the pain pills seemed to have taken care of that.

Mitzi was glad Annie insisted Heather ride with her and that Kelly had climbed into the Hummer. That way Keith had no distractions. Their convoy descended the mountain in reverse order, with the Hummer out in front.

It was after nine o'clock Sunday night by the time they got everyone home and cars switched back. Dan insisted on being their last stop. Annie parked the Bronco in his drive and Mitzi pulled in behind her. Keith had followed them so Annie would have her car back once she drove him home. Bruce was still dropping off the last of the kids.

That left the three of them to get Dan inside. The pain meds made him loopy, so the crutches were out of the question. Getting him into the wheelchair was no easier, and once they had him situated they still needed to get him up the front step and into his house.

It was Keith who thought to look in the garage for a piece of plywood to make a ramp of sorts. And Keith who helped Dan from the wheelchair to the couch before he and Annie left.

It seemed wrong to leave Dan alone in his condition, so she called her dad to let him know where she was spending the night. "Can I get you anything?" she asked, closing her cell phone. "Some extra pillows?"

"That would be nice."

He directed her toward his bedroom and she brought out two more pillows. Mitzi eased the first one under his leg. A couple of the girls had had multicolored markers with them, and his cast had taken on its own personality.

He leaned forward so she could sit behind him. She settled the pillow and his head in her lap and handed him the remote.

"This is my idea of heaven," he said, flipping through the channels while she stroked his dark brown hair. "I'm sorry I screwed up our time together."

"I wouldn't say that," she said. "You gave the kids something to talk about. And at least it happened on the last run of the day."

"No, I meant our time." His glance swept her face, then toward his cast. "I'm going to be out of commission for a while."

He reached up to pull her head down for a kiss. Apparently out of commission didn't mean completely out of action. His hand slipped beneath her blouse. As he worked his way up her rib cage to cup her breast, she realized two things. That she had just experienced arousal at the hands of another man. And that she had always, always been faithful to Calhoun.

She was afraid her inexperience with other men showed. When Danny moved beyond her comfort zone to unhook her bra and cup her bare breast, she tried to think of ways to slow him down without totally turning him off.

She gasped as he raised her blouse and took the peak of one breast into his mouth.

"Just a taste," he said, pulling back. "I don't want to scare you off." He covered her back up and she fell a little in love with him.

"Danny Estrada, you are one sweet, sweet man."

"I'm afraid my self-restraint is in question

tonight," he confessed, indicating the prescription bottle on his coffee table.

It was just around ten o'clock when his doorbell rang.

"Who do you suppose that is?" she asked. Dan raised himself from her lap so she could get up to answer it.

"I'll give you one guess," he said.

"Calhoun," she said, using the peephole. Mitzi opened the door.

"Impeccable timing, as always," Dan said. Mitzi felt the immediate undercurrent that was always there between the two men.

"What are you doing here?" she asked.

"Thought Estrada could use my help."

"I'm here."

"If you're okay with getting him to the bathroom." She hadn't thought about that. "Otherwise I'm spending the night," he said, throwing his jacket onto a nearby chair and sitting down.

"We're all right together," Dan reassured her. "Why don't you head home and get some sleep?"

"If you're sure…"

"I'm just going to crash anyway."

Mitzi picked up her shoulder bag and jacket. "Good night," she said.

"You might want to adjust yourself first," Calhoun said, making her aware that her bra was still unhooked.

She waited until she was outside in the van to *adjust* herself.

"ARE YOU JUST GOING TO sit there and glare at me all night?" Estrada asked. They were watching late-night TV on Comedy Central, neither one of them saying much.

"I might," Bruce admitted. "I'm trying to figure out a polite way of putting this. So here it is." He looked Estrada in the eye. "You hurt her, and next time I don't just break your leg in two places, I break your neck."

"Fair enough," the other man said.

Bruce hadn't literally broken the other man's leg. But their competition down the mountain had gotten out of hand.

"That was some pretty awesome flat lining for a gimp," Estrada said. When flat lining on a steep slope there was always that point of no return.

No slowing down, no stopping.

Where any attempt to turn or check your speed resulted in a crash. You just had to hold on until you reached the bottom. That's all Bruce had done. With sheer grit and determination he'd held on longer than the other man.

But there was such a thing as holding on too tight.

Bruce reached into his back pocket for his wallet. He pulled out two tickets to *The Nutcracker.* "She gave up her opening-night tickets, but she likes ballet. And this is her favorite." He tossed the tickets to the coffee table.

NOVEMBER HAD COME AND GONE. Though it seemed like only yesterday that he'd walked through that door of the recruiting office, he'd been here a month. As Bruce hung up the phone his gaze drifted toward Mitzi.

She and Henry were getting ready to go to the VA. Henry was still trying to hide his training leg from her with a lap blanket. Bruce shook his head.

"What?" she asked. "You're staring."

The call was the one he'd been waiting for.

O-course, next week. He'd been thinking he'd hear something after Christmas. Physically he was up to the challenge. He just wasn't mentally prepared for it to be this soon.

"The Parade of Lights is this weekend," he said. "I volunteered to help Lucky with the Toys for Tots float. I was wondering if you'd like to come?"

"Dan and I have parade plans both nights." She worried her bottom lip. "We're taking in the parade, then having dinner downtown." He pursed his lips and nodded in acceptance of the situation. He told himself it was for the best now that his departure was imminent.

"What about you, old man?"

"Got bells to ring."

Looked as if he was going alone.

"Do you need help with the float?" she asked, throwing him a bone. "Before Friday, I mean."

"If your idea of fun is chicken wire and tissue paper. Tonight and tomorrow night."

"I think a Parade of Lights float is a little more sophisticated than high school homecoming, Calhoun," she said, getting up from her desk with car keys in hand. "What time?"

"Right after work. I'll pick you up."

THE *NUTCRACKER*-THEMED FLOAT sponsored by Toys for Tots and Build a Bear had arrived at the staging warehouse on that Wednesday before the Friday/Saturday parade—in pieces.

Some assembly required would have been an understatement.

Mitzi's mission had been to make sure everyone had enough black coffee to keep them going. Bruce, Lucky and another half dozen Marines from Lucky's reserve unit had spent the next forty-eight hours putting the float together in shifts.

Somehow Mitzi had let Lucky rope her into playing Clara for the second year in a row. Dan had more than understood—he'd volunteered along with everyone else.

The slight modification to their plans gave them the full parade experience for the two-day televised event sponsored by 9NEWS. Huddled in the staging area on Friday, waiting for the parade to begin, other costumed characters like her were surrounded by festive balloons, high-school marching bands and horse-drawn carriages.

The worst part was knowing she was about to freeze her tutu off. Just as soon as she removed her jacket.

"Hi," Dan said, rolling up in his wheelchair. He had a cast on his left leg, from his foot halfway up his thigh. He'd broken his leg in two places. She wasn't quite sure what had happened that day, only that Bruce and Dan were in a race to the bottom.

She bent to kiss him. "How's the leg?"

"Itchy."

"I need you to put this on." Lucky, dressed as a very fit-looking Marine Corps Santa Claus, held out an oversize Rat King head to Bruce, complete with crown.

"You're kidding, right?"

Dan snickered.

"Not kidding." He forced the rat head into Bruce's hands. "Sorry, Mitzi," Lucky said, "the coat's gotta come off. I found this for you." He handed her a short cape, pink with white faux fur trim, that would cover her shoulders. He did provide her with two pairs of long-sleeved pink tights to wear under her tutu.

"Break a leg," Dan teased as she handed him her coat for safekeeping. "I'll meet you at the finish line." Which was right back here where they were starting. She smiled at him.

Bruce removed his white service cap and put the Rat King head on. "At least it's warm in here." His voice echoed.

Mitzi helped him with his white web belt and sword because he couldn't see well enough to do it on his own. "You look quite dashing, Your Highness. For a rat."

"Aren't I supposed to be the bad guy in all this, Meredith Marie?" For as long as she could remember she'd been going by Mitzi, or Mitz for short. It was so much a part of her, she'd almost forgotten who'd given her those nicknames.

It had started with Bruce teasing her with "Mini-Marie" at six. By the time school started she was Mitzi.

"How could you ever be the bad guy, Bruce?" She checked his gig line, making sure all his buttons were aligned. Her hand came to rest on his chest and he covered her hand with his gloved hand.

"Dear sweet Marie…" He began to recite from *The Nutcracker* and she stopped him.

"I think we're about to begin."

FOR THE SECOND NIGHT in a row Marines in dress blues marched alongside the float, while the Englewood High School marching band moved out in front, playing "Here Comes Santa Claus."

That tune was going to be stuck in his head for days.

If it wasn't for his high and tight, his hair would have been matted. As it was, Bruce was dripping with sweat when he removed his Rat King head.

At the end of the parade route marching bands dispersed and floats were towed back to warehouses for the night. He still had a long night ahead of him and another long day tomorrow, helping to disassemble the thing for storage. But all in all he'd enjoyed the experience.

Now warm beneath her overcoat, Mitzi huddled over steaming hot cocoa with the other volunteers. Her cheeks were pink from the cold. And he had the strongest desire to kiss the tip of her nose to see if it was just as cold.

"You look ready to call it a night," he said.

"I am." She picked up a cup of cocoa from the volunteer station and handed it to him.

"No dinner date with Dan this evening?"

"He's pulling the car around. In his condition

and with this crowd he could be a while. At least it's his left leg—" She cut herself off abruptly. "I'm s-sorry," she stammered. "I didn't mean—"

"I know what you meant, Chief."

She hid from further embarrassment behind a sip of cocoa.

He wasn't embarrassed. His left leg was gone. He'd rather talk about it than shy away from it. And yet here he was having trouble spitting out the very words he'd been waiting to say to her since his arrival. "I'm leaving, come Monday."

She stared at him over the brim of her cup. "Before Christmas?"

He nodded.

His duty assignment would follow. But he was thinking of using some of his leave to ensure he'd be home for Christmas.

He hadn't been home for Christmas in a long time.

He surprised them both by giving in to the urge and kissing the tip of her cherry nose. "Good night," he said as if it wasn't goodbye.

It was as cold as it looked.

Bruce couldn't help but smile when he realized her eyes remained on him as he headed back toward the warehouse.

Not far from where the parade had begun and ended, he spotted his brother's car in a nearly empty lot. Keith was standing beside it in his Build a Bear costume, holding his bear head to his hip.

Kelly, in her blue-and-white band uniform with her snare drum hanging from the strap around her neck, gestured wildly with her drumsticks and appeared to be giving Keith an earful.

Bruce couldn't hear.

But he was pretty sure Keith deserved it.

Kelly stormed off in tears toward the relative safety of the volunteer station. Keith got into his car, slamming the door before he drove away.

Young love. What a pain in the ass.

CHAPTER FOURTEEN

A WOMAN WALKED into the lounge on Sunday and Mitzi looked up from wiping down the bar. "Audrey!"

"Do you like it?" she asked, turning in a slow circle so Mitzi could get the full effect of her makeover. "I was watching *What Not to Wear* and realized they were talking about my entire wardrobe."

"I love it," Mitzi said.

"Do you mind if I borrow your dad? My car stalled out on me not too far from here. I was hoping he could come take a look."

"Dad's really good with cars." But then, Audrey knew that. She was glad the woman had decided to fight Nora Jean for him. "And I bet he would appreciate a home-cooked meal in return." Audrey was a good cook and Mitzi knew for a fact Nora Jean didn't know her way around a kitchen.

"Right—dinner," Audrey said, catching on quickly.

"Wait." Mitzi leaned over the bar and unbuttoned the other woman's top button. Audrey gasped, but Mitzi was pleased with the result. "You might want to tell him you were headed out on a date when your car broke down. It will make you seem unavailable."

"Do I want to seem unavailable?" Audrey asked.

"Oh, yeah," Mitzi said. "Just don't play too hard to get."

With that advice Audrey went in search of Mitzi's father. A few minutes later he came into the bar. "I'm gonna go help Audrey. Do you think you can close up for the night?"

"Not a problem."

As they were leaving she heard her father say, "Where did you say you met this fella?"

"Online?" Audrey said, making it sound more like a question.

Mitzi finished wiping down the table with a smile on her face. Restaurants and bars were allowed to sell alcohol on Sunday in Colorado. The Broadway Bar & Bowl was no exception, but it still closed at six on Sundays.

It was almost that now.

She sent the staff home on the dot, then went around locking doors and turning out lights. She heard music and realized it was coming from the arcade.

She'd already turned out the lights in the arcade.

Her dad kept a gun on the premises—he was a retired cop—but it was locked in the safe. Along with a lot of cash. She grabbed a bottle of whiskey in one hand and her cell phone in the other and went to investigate.

Tashannie's "Caution (Don't Bother Me)" was a real favorite of the "DDR" pumpers, the kids who put a lot of energy into their "Dance Dance Revolution" game. Judging by the number of times she'd heard it in passing this evening, she had a real diehard on her hands.

When she crossed the threshold from the bowling alley to the arcade, she was surprised to see Calhoun was the pumper. He wasn't dancing, really. But he was up on the platform of the "Dance Dance Revolution" game, trying to keep up with the lights.

He was so focused on his feet he didn't even notice her. She leaned back against the arch and watched. Was there nothing that man wouldn't try?

He sure didn't let a little thing like a missing leg hold him back. She admired that about him. She waited to clap until the song ended.

"Nice Riverdance there, Gunny."

He whipped around, embarrassed. "You weren't supposed to see that."

"You just need practice." She moved toward the "DDR" machine and ducked under the bar to join him on the platform. "Try it again."

He shook his head. "I was just trying to keep out of your way until you were ready to close."

He'd looked as if he really wanted to master this machine.

"I'm not busy now. And there's nobody here but us," she said, looking around. "Come on, try it with me."

She fed the coins into the slot when he wouldn't.

"If you can do jumping jacks, Marine, you can handle this machine. Just remember you have four arrows shoulder width—two sides, front and back. Start out feet together—" she demonstrated "—now shoulder width. See, a jumping jack." She did it again, and this time he did it with her. "Now add a turn. Feet together, shoulder width, hop/turn, shoulder width. Again…" she repeated until they'd made a circle. "Other direction. Now front and back…"

Once he had those few basic moves down, he was ready for music. She made her selection and "Caution (Don't Bother Me)" started again. "Look at the screen, not at your feet," she said, showing him the arrows with the steps he needed to follow. "Memorize these patterns. That's what the pumpers do. After you learn a song you won't even need the screen."

He missed a beat. "Jumping jack, turn," she called out to get him back on track. "Now you're getting the hang of it. Add your hips. Your shoulders."

He relaxed enough to have fun, and they were laughing together after a few songs.

"So tomorrow's the big day?"

He nodded. "I fly out in the morning."

That's it? No goodbye? Just this awkward moment to remember him by?

Her throat closed around everything she wanted to say right now.

"How 'bout we slow it down?" she suggested.

She chose Ne-Yo's "Closer" and danced just for him.

She tapped every light on both sides of the game with some very un-jumping-jack-like moves. Her eyes never left his as she rolled her hips. Her shoulders.

He leaned back against the screen to watch.

She untied and unwound the bar apron she was wearing over a sweater and jeans and tossed it over the side of the platform. Then she unbuttoned all but the one button at her breast to flash him some skin.

As the song ended, Mitzi dropped to her knees. "Hit it again," she said.

He did.

And she gave up all pretense of dancing.

"Mitzi—" He started to protest.

She gripped his thighs. "I'm calling your bluff, Calhoun." She ran her hands up the backs of his legs. On the right there was flesh and bone beneath the denim. On the left the hard shell of his socket. She slid both hands up to cup his ass. "Tell me you don't want this," she said, her palm riding his erection through his jeans all the way up his button fly.

His answer was to brush the hair back from her mouth and free her ponytail. Tangling his hand in her hair he brought them both closer to where they wanted to be.

Mitzi didn't need any more encouragement than that.

She unbuttoned his jeans from the top button down. Slipping her hand inside his open fly, she felt his heat beneath the cotton of his boxer briefs. She wrapped her hand around the length of him, using the friction of the thin material to draw out her slow seduction.

She traced the line of flesh along his elastic waistband to the head of his erection. She slid her fingers beneath the band and freed him from his briefs.

He threw his head back against the machine as she touched him skin to skin. She drew out his torture with slow strokes before bringing her mouth close enough to trace the head of his penis with her tongue. When a taste was no longer enough to satisfy either of them, she closed her mouth over him.

He gripped her head in both hands and groaned.

BRUCE TUGGED Mitzi's head back. She looked up at him through her long lashes. "I'm not done," she said sweetly.

Could he be any more turned on?

"I want to return the favor," he growled.

"Oh," she said, teasing him, "why didn't you say so?"

"I thought I just did." He pulled her up by the hair none too gently. His mouth came down hard on hers. He had her back against the rail and wasn't letting up. He tasted the warm, wet heat of her mouth—her mouth that had been on him.

He deepened their kiss, demanding more.

Lifting her to the rail, he spread her legs wide, pressed her to him. She clung to him, answering his demands with demands of her own.

He had a hand on her thigh, working the inseam of her jeans with his thumb. There'd been a lot of "clothes on" make-out sessions when they were younger and he knew just where to rub to really turn her on.

Sliding his other hand up her rib cage, he cupped her breast over her bra. She moaned into his mouth.

Her hand slipped back into his jeans and he had to reach for her hand to stop her. He wanted to drag this out as long as possible.

Lifting her off the rail, he wrapped her legs around his waist and headed for the pool table. Fred was going to kill him. Then again, he'd be living one of his top ten fantasies.

They'd just never had the opportunity before.

He laid her back on the green felt. He stood over her for a moment, then very deliberately unbuttoned her jeans as she lay there looking up at him.

He didn't break eye contact as he lowered her zipper.

She lifted her hips, inviting him to pull her jeans past her bottom. He paused to remove her shoes. He took a heel of each shoe in his hands and dropped them to the floor.

He left her socks on.

He got back to the business of removing her jeans, which meant he had to step from between her legs to pull them off and toss them aside.

He left her panties on.

Navy blue, stretch lace with a peach bow, and wet to his touch.

The moment he touched her beneath the lace, she threw her head back and arched into his hand.

Cupping her bottom in both hands, he positioned

her so he could get a better angle for what he was about to do next.

Murmuring words of encouragement, he lowered his mouth to taste her with his tongue.

MITZI BUCKED BENEATH HIM.

Her climax came hard, and like a wave crashing against the shore, again and again. He lifted his head with a satisfied smile on his face.

She couldn't have erased the smile from her own face if she'd tried. He could be as smug as he liked.

He dragged her back toward him. She pushed his unbuttoned jeans past his hips. And grabbed two fistfuls of that hot ass of his.

She wrapped her legs around his thighs as he settled between hers. She reached for his shirt to unbutton it. Before she'd finished, he'd unbuttoned his cuffs and lifted both his shirt and T-shirt off over his head.

While he tossed them aside, she admired all that hard muscle. Running her hands over his shoulders and chest, she followed with soft kisses.

Shrugging out of her unbuttoned sweater, she watched as he bent his head to her breasts. He pushed them up out of her push-up bra and gave her aching nipples all his attention.

Her bra straps fell from her shoulders, but her

bra stayed on. He stretched the leg hole of her panties aside to enter her.

They'd always been a tight fit, but she was more than ready for that first thrust. And the next. And the next.

She pressed a kiss to his neck and he lifted his head. She pressed a soft kiss to his lips, tasted herself there and kissed him again. And again.

He deepened the kiss without demand this time.

A soft exploration, encouraging her to explore.

He murmured endearments against her mouth.

Her neck. Her shoulders.

Her breasts.

And when he came, he filled her completely.

BRUCE HITCHED HIS PANTS back up around his hips and buttoned his fly. He didn't want this night to end in awkwardness, so he was careful to take his time getting dressed.

"I'd invite you back to my place," he teased, "but my mother might have something to say about that."

"It's okay," she said, buttoning her sweater.

"Not okay," he said, stopping her so she had to look at him. "I want to spend the night with you."

She had a pink tinge to her cheeks. Was she embarrassed by this? Was she thinking about Dan? He certainly wasn't.

He leaned in and kissed her again.

She pushed against his chest. "You don't want my dad to come looking for me."

"Not if it means explaining why he might want to re-cover his pool table."

"What he doesn't know won't hurt him," she agreed.

"We could go somewhere," he suggested.

"Somewhere, like where?"

"Like anywhere with a bed."

CHAPTER FIFTEEN

MITZI DIDN'T KNOW how they got to the motel. Other than he drove her car. She didn't know how they'd gotten most of their clothes off the minute they'd stepped inside the door. Other than his hands were all over her. And her hands were all over him.

Suddenly she realized they were in the same motel they used to sneak off to as kids. Spending the night with Calhoun was a bad idea at best. Spending the night with him here, well, that was heartbreak waiting to happen. They'd said their goodbyes tonight. What was the point of prolonging the inevitable?

"Wait," she said against his lips. "Don't you... want to take your pants off? And your leg?"

They were face-to-face. He was sitting on the bed with his shirt off and his pants unzipped. And she was straddling his lap in her bra and panties.

"Do you want me to take my leg off?"

She swallowed past the catch in her throat. "I

don't even know how it stays on." She touched his face.

"It stays on with suction and it doesn't come off until you're ready."

She nodded. This had been a long time coming. But now that the moment was here, she felt apprehensive. She could tell he did, too. What did he have to feel nervous about? He took his leg off every night and put it back on every morning.

She slid off his lap and sat next to him on the bed. He didn't take his pants off standing up anymore, but sitting down. He had them halfway down his thighs before he bent to take off his shoes and socks. He took the right ones off first.

"I don't always take the left shoe off," he said. "Sometimes it's just easier to take the leg off."

The artificial foot was the only part of his leg fashioned to look the way it should. He finished taking his pants off. She'd gotten glimpses of his leg before, but had never seen the silicone socket that covered his stump. It was cut low on the inseam and high on his hip.

"The length is for stability," he said. He depressed a button near a valve at the bottom of the socket to release the vacuum.

She sucked in her breath.

He had to gently rock the suction socket back and forth until he'd freed himself. Red and pinched from the tight fit, surprisingly, what was left of his leg was hairless. She didn't know if hair just didn't grow there anymore or if the leg had been worn smooth by the socket. But she was glad to see his surgical scars had healed.

He leaned his leg against the nightstand. If it was that tight coming off… "How do you get it back on?"

His jaw tightened. "Well, that's going to be a problem. I didn't bring a donning sock. But I'll manage." He reached for his leg, but she reached it first.

"Get over yourself, Calhoun," she said. "I wasn't asking you to put it back on. Just curious. I might have something you could use, though." Her purse had wound up on the nightstand and she pulled out a knee-high stocking. "It has a run in it." She stretched it out for his inspection.

"That'll do."

Tucking it into the socket, she set his leg back where he'd put it. He grabbed her hand and pulled her back to him.

"It would feel really good right now, Mitzi, if you touched me," he said. "I usually massage the stump when the leg comes off."

"I can do that," she said, surprised by the huskiness of her own voice.

He closed a firm hand over hers. "Not too light. Otherwise it feels like pins and needles. Nerves take a long time to recover. If ever."

She increased the pressure. "How does that feel?"

"You can't even imagine." His voice filled with desire. Eyes closed. Breathing shallow. Legs touching. He had his hand along her inner thigh.

When he dropped his head in his hand, breathing labored, she mistook it for excitement. Simply because she was about to come again from his touch. Then she realized his hand on her thigh had stilled and his shoulders were shaking. "Bruce," she said softly.

"We were this close. Our thighs bumping up against each other... I should have sat on his left. I should have sat on his left," he repeated, his voice strained.

If he started crying, she'd start crying.

"Don't you dare," she warned, "*ever think* I would trade one of you for the other. You were meant to be in this moment, Bruce. Please don't feel guilty about that." Her voice was barely above a whisper.

When he looked up his face was wet. And when their lips met she tasted the salt of his grief for her brother. Laying her back on the bed, he kissed her. He took his time stripping her underwear and slipping off his boxer briefs. He stared into her eyes, gauging her reaction as he spread her thighs with his stump.

And entered her.

BRUCE STOOD with his hand on the doorknob debating whether or not to wake her before he left. They'd made love till near exhaustion and, if he had to leave, this is how he wanted to remember her.

She was lying on her stomach. Her bare back and lower legs exposed by the rumpled sheets. Head turned away from him into the pillow.

The motel room didn't look any better in the predawn hours than it had last night. He should have taken her someplace nice. But this was where they'd gone all the way that first time.

He took one last look around the room.

She'd given him a gift. What could he give her in return? The promise he'd leave her again and again?

Last night had been about letting go. She was ready to move on.

And he had to let her.

MITZI WAITED until Calhoun closed the door with a quiet click before she sat up. She reached for the knee-high stocking he'd left on the bed and twisted it around her hands.

Now what?

She never should have let him take her heart with him.

At the same time, she couldn't regret one minute of their last night together.

HENRY ROLLED IN around his usual time on Wednesday. Mitzi was glad to see he had a nice warm lap blanket to cover himself. But if he thought he was hiding his legs from her, he was mistaken.

She'd also noticed that since Bruce had cleaned Henry up, first with a haircut, then later helping him to a shower in their locker room, Henry was taking more pride in his appearance.

"You ready?" Mitzi asked, grabbing her handbag.

"Don't need a ride," he said. "Got regular scheduled appointments now. See a physical therapist three days a week, too."

"Oh?" That *was* good news.

"Boy's got my back," Henry said, nodding toward Calhoun's empty desk. "Just wanted to bring you this early Christmas present." He reached under his blanket and pulled out an ornament. "Good stuff left over after the Parade of Lights."

He handed over the ornament. The small nutcracker had a blue coat with red piping. He looked just like a little Marine. But the thing that made him extra special was that his left leg had been splintered off at the knee.

Most people would look at the broken nutcracker and see trash. Henry looked at trash and saw more than most people.

"Thank you, Henry," she said past the lump in her throat. "I will cherish him forever."

Henry shrugged off her thanks. "Figured he was too good to just throw away." Using his hands, he manipulated the wheels to back up. "Got another surprise for you closer to Christmas," he said, making that vague promise before he left.

For her part Mitzi hoped the duplex was move-in ready by then. Henry had given her a deposit toward his rent weeks ago. She didn't know how he'd come up with the cash between disability checks, but he'd been flashing a lot of large bills lately. The only reason she'd agreed to take the money from him was to lock it up in her desk and keep him from being jumped for it.

Mitzi stood the nutcracker next to the picture on her desk. His stand was still attached by his one good leg. She hadn't even started her holiday shopping and had no idea what she was going to get anyone for Christmas.

Mitzi took a deep breath and checked her calendar. Aside from an appointment with her CO later that afternoon, she had nothing for the rest of the week. Because she hadn't committed one way or the other, her commanding officer wanted to give her the reenlistment pep talk.

She left to get in a couple hours of shopping downtown, where she found something for everyone on her Christmas list. Except Calhoun.

On the way back to the office she stopped by her newly renovated duplex. The painters were adding the finishing touches before furnishings were moved back in. It was there in the house she'd bought with Freddie's endowment that she realized exactly what she wanted to give Bruce for Christmas.

Not that she'd actually give it to him.

MITZI ARRANGED TO MEET Dan at the Broadway Bar & Bowl after work. He rolled in just after four o'clock. He was still in a wheelchair, but he was starting to use his crutches more and carried them around with him. He was even driving again, since the Bronco was an automatic transmission and he needed only his right foot to work the gas and brakes.

"Hi," Dan said with his dimpled grin.

Mitzi bent to kiss him on the cheek. She'd had a hard time looking Dan in the eye since she and Calhoun had done what they'd done. Especially since Dan had started to feel better, hinting that his cast had not completely incapacitated him.

That only served to remind Mitzi of a time when Bruce was still in his wheelchair and she'd tried to get his attention by straddling him. He'd rebuked her then.

She and Dan sat at a table in the darkened lounge and ordered a couple of beers and a platter of nachos. From where Mitzi sat she had a clear view of the game room.

"Long day?" he asked.

"Hmm?" She forced herself to focus as their server set beers in front of them.

"The rest of your order will be out shortly," the young woman said. "Is there anything else I can get you?"

"No, thank you," Mitzi said and the young woman left them alone again.

"You keep rubbing your neck," Dan commented. "Do you have a headache?"

"Oh, no," she said, putting her hand down on the table. "I just had a meeting with my CO today. My enlistment is up shortly, and he's trying to talk me into reenlisting. There's a nice bonus if I return to SAR as a rescue swimmer. Or he offered me two more years here—" thanks to her meeting her quota with Keith Calhoun "—if I want to stick with recruiting."

Leaning forward, he covered her hand with his. "Whether you decide to reenlist or not, I hope you'll stay in Colorado."

"Dan—" she rubbed the back of her neck again "—I need to tell you something."

"Is this about Calhoun?"

"It's not what you think. Well, maybe it is…it didn't mean anything, just goodbye."

"You slept with him?" Dan recoiled back in his chair. "That's a whole lot worse than what I was thinking."

"I'm just trying to be honest. I thought you'd—"

He cut her off, lifting his hand to stop her. "I mean it's not like we…" He sighed heavily. "I've been very patient, Mitzi." He dug out his wallet and threw a couple of bills to the center of the table. He added a pair of tickets.

She picked up *The Nutcracker* tickets, a last reminder of how thoughtful Dan was. "Maybe once you…see past what I did—"

"Maybe," he said, struggling to maneuver his wheelchair toward the door.

Mitzi sat there for a while wondering why she felt so relieved. Then she ate the whole platter of nachos. And she didn't feel so good.

THE USMC O-COURSE WAS a matter of pride.

All Marines were required to pass a semiannual physical fitness test, and Bruce was no exception. The test had been conducted in a single session over two hours with minimum requirements for pull-ups, crunches and a three-mile run. With his entire Force Recon unit turning out to offer support and cheer him on, Bruce had passed with flying colors.

But every Marine knew the real test started in the pit with fifty yards of Lincoln Log-style structures stretched out before him. And a rope to climb at the end. The obstacle course wasn't a timed event, even though every Marine knew his best time.

And tried to beat it.

Marines gave up weekend liberty to practice getting over The Wall. And the fate of a recruit might rest on how well his drill instructor or captain felt he'd done on the O-course. Anything under two minutes was respectable.

Just getting through it the first dozen or so times was a challenge, but Bruce had ten years of practice. Today he intended to beat his personal best, which stood as the unit record—1:05.

Captain Horton held the stopwatch. "Ready?"

Bruce had stripped down to his T-shirt and camouflage pants. Boots. Bouncing on his toes, Bruce nodded.

AFTER HIS PHYSICAL FITNESS test and O-course, Bruce stood at attention outside the major's office. Captain Horton left carrying Bruce's personnel file and nodded for him to follow.

"At ease," Horton said as he rounded his desk. "Nice job out there today, Calhoun. Welcome back."

"Thank you, sir." Bruce shifted from attention to at rest with his feet apart and hands behind his back.

"The major has asked me to pass along his congratulations in setting a new unit record on the

O-course today." Bruce nodded as the captain closed his file and tossed it to the desk. "I'm supposed to have you initial off on your options before the reenlistment ceremony. Personnel went over your bonuses with you?"

"Yes, sir." Bruce, and Freddie for that matter, had been Stop Loss retentions, meaning they wouldn't be let out of their enlistment contracts because of a shortage of personnel.

His actual enlistment had ended two years ago.

"Here it is," Horton said. "Number one—you can walk away now with an honorable discharge and monthly disability checks."

Bruce stiffened.

"Yeah, didn't think you'd like that one." The captain studied him for a moment. "You know option two. All you have to do is make it official. But apparently you're a damn fine recruiter, Calhoun. And Lieutenant Colonel Avari back in Colorado thinks mighty highly of you. That's option number three."

"Thank you, sir."

"Your recruiting numbers speak for themselves. So before we get you sworn in for another four years, Calhoun, which will it be?"

CHAPTER SIXTEEN

ON FRIDAY MORNING Mitzi drove Keith Calhoun downtown to the Military Entrance Processing Station in the old U.S. Custom House building. Keith had reached the point of no return in his enlistment.

"No Recruiters Beyond This Point."

Mitzi paced the hall while Keith spoke with the detailer, signing the contract that would bind him to the United States Navy for the next four to six years. She'd explained each step of the process carefully, but from here on out, the choices were his and his alone.

As were the choices she'd had to make.

He wasn't the only one raising his right hand today.

Keith stepped back into the hall. "You ready?"

"Please repeat after me," the officer at the podium said to the dozen or so young men and women in civilian clothes, standing in loose formation. Many with family and friends in attendance.

"I, *state your name*—" names were stated "—do solemnly swear (or affirm) that I will support and defend the Constitution of the United States against all enemies, foreign and domestic; that I will bear true faith and allegiance to the same; and that I will obey the orders of the president of the United States and the orders of the officers appointed over me, according to regulations and the Uniform Code of Military Justice. So help me God."

"Should we hug or shake hands? Or something?" Keith asked when the brief ceremony was over.

"We can do that."

He held out his hand. She smiled and pulled him into her arms.

Maybe if she could have seen over his shoulder she would have had more warning. When they pulled back, Bruce was standing outside the doorway.

What was he doing here?

He looked at Keith, looked at her and came to his own conclusions. Without a word to either of them, he left.

Mitzi followed him to the elevator. He took the stairs.

She followed him down. "Would you just give me a chance to explain?" She had to run to keep up.

"You had a chance to explain." He pushed through the exit to the street. Calhoun's military bearing was too ingrained for him to start a fight outside the customs building. Or anywhere in public, for that matter. "Were numbers that important to you? My brother is not just another recruit."

"I don't feel that way about any of my kids."

"You should have come to me when he first came to you."

"He didn't want me to."

"I could have talked some sense into him."

"Yeah, well, that wasn't working out so well. Have you even read his paper on Iwo Jima? I left a copy on your desk. He wants this. He wants it as much as you."

"How long?"

"Since his ASVAB scores came out."

"So practically the whole time we've been working together you've been working behind my back?"

MITZI DROVE KEITH HOME in silence. There was a dark red—maybe maroon—SUV in the shared drive. A brand-new Ford Escalade. She pulled into her father's half of the driveway and parked.

"Do you want me to come in with you?"

"You don't have to," he said. "I'm sure Bruce has already told them."

"Does he know about Heather?"

"Do you think that will make a difference?" He perked up.

"No," she said. "A pregnant girlfriend is not likely to be the answer to all your problems."

"Lucky knows," he said, spotting his brother's motorcycle on the street. "We had a long talk when I told him. At least he won't let Bruce kill me. I don't know, maybe he knows already. He's been trying to get me to open up about things."

Everyone was talking at once when they walked into the kitchen. Clearly the family was divided. Keith's dad, John, and Lucky seemed to be of one mind. While Bruce and Keith's mom, Eva, seemed to be of another.

They all turned on Keith.

"I joined the Navy," he announced. "I leave for boot camp after graduation. And when I get back, Heather and I are getting married. We're having a baby." He plucked an apple from a bowl of fruit. "I'm going to my room. I'm grounded for life, whatever. I'll be out of your hair by June."

Bruce leaned against the counter with his arms crossed. Mitzi could tell by the expression on his face that Heather's pregnancy didn't let her off the hook, either.

"I'll be in my room, too," she said, "if any-body wants me." *Please, let him still want me.* Nobody except Bruce was paying any attention to her when she left to cross the drive to her father's house and go up to her room.

BRUCE NEVER SHOWED UP at the office the next morning, although both his vehicles were parked out back. He didn't show at his parents' home that evening, where plenty was going on since Keith had broken the news of his enlistment.

Followed by the news of Heather's pregnancy.

Mitzi dropped by the bowling alley. The gym.

Anywhere she thought Calhoun might be.

She waited up half the night at her father's house in hopes of hearing some indication of his return. Finally she picked up the phone and said all those things she wished she'd said. Then called him back and told him to ignore half of what she'd said. "I'm sorry, I was wrong not to tell you. I have your back, Calhoun. Please, call me back."

The next day she stuck to her plan of moving back into her place. Mostly because she'd already arranged to meet Henry there and give him his key.

When she arrived, Henry was out front. If she'd hoped to see Calhoun there with him she was sorely disappointed.

Henry had a single box in his lap for his move.

Mitzi had furnished his half of the duplex for him with secondhand furniture from several thrift stores. Not a half-bad decorating job at that.

She presented him with the key.

"Now this makes you my landlord," he said. "I have every intention of paying you my rent. On time. Every month."

She wheeled him toward the ramp.

"Stop!" he ordered at the bottom of the ramp. "Told you I had another Christmas present for you."

"You can give it to me inside. It's cold out here."

Who moved in December anyway?

But he tossed aside his lap blanket to reveal his gait training leg. "When did you get that?" she asked. But she wasn't surprised.

"Had it a couple weeks," he said proudly. "Been practicing. Physical therapy. And on my own." He set the brake on his wheelchair and pushed to his feet. He grabbed the handrail for support. Then slowly, very slowly, he put one foot in front of the other all the way to his own front door.

Mitzi applauded.

If he hadn't looked so fragile she would have hugged him. *What the hell!* She hugged him anyway. As far as she knew a hug never killed anybody. "Would you like to go to *The Nutcracker* with me?"

HIS BEARD ITCHED. And Bruce wasn't talking about the fake Santa one either, but the stubble underneath the faux white beard. And that was only a week without a shave.

He'd gotten what he deserved. He'd taken the recruiting assignment, obviously. Reenlisted. Bought a minivan, or close enough, with his 35K. Had driven all the way back from California with a pair of red cowgirl boots on the passenger seat.

To prove to her that he was ready to settle down. Maybe not the exact kind of settled she saw for their future, but a compromise.

He should have learned his lesson the first time.

Then Lucky had called. Cait had gone into labor.

And "backup" Santa had been pressed into service.

There were over fifty thousand toys to hand out, so the line at the high-school auditorium seemed never ending. Okay, he didn't have to hand them all out. Only to the kids who wanted to see Santa. He'd been spit up on, spit on, hit—and hit on by one hot mama—and peed on... Not to mention kicked in the shin more times than he could count.

"Aim for the left one next time," he said to one particularly vicious six-year-old girl. And she did.

"You're not the real Santa," she said. "You're the Marine Corps Santa."

"Yeah, so?" She couldn't tell that by his lack of padding? "Take your doll and go."

"So if you were the real Santa you'd know what I want for Christmas."

"What's that, G.I. Joe?"

"I want my mom home from Iraq. She was supposed to be home, but they made her stay."

"I'm sorry," he said, with sincerity this time. "I know she misses you and would be here with you if she could." And then tears and another kick to his good shin. The girl's grandmother apologized and took her away.

Bruce decided it was time for a break. And that's when Keith found him. In the teachers' lounge, icing down his battered and bruised shin, in his Santa suit.

"I tried to tell you about Heather," Keith said.

"You told me you weren't sleeping with her."

"It's complicated."

"Yeah," Bruce agreed.

Keith was silent a moment. "We're getting married right after I get out of boot camp. Mitzi said it would be easier if I went in without dependents."

"Yeah, I'll bet she did. From not dating to married, pretty big leap." Keith looked miserable, as he should. If he'd opened up they could have discussed his brother's options. As it was, Keith was paying for one mistake by making a couple more.

"You might want to get over being mad sooner

rather than later. She pretty much figured you'd passed the O-course. She reenlisted because she plans to head back to Iraq or Afghanistan or wherever."

Why would she do that? For the same reason he'd buy an SUV. And a pair of red boots. The same reason he took his hometown recruiting assignment.

"Lose something, Calhoun?" the wheel-chair bound coach asked, muscling in on their conversation.

But he knew where he could find her. "I need those ballet tickets, Estrada."

"Why would I give them to you?" Dan pushed open the door of the teachers' lounge. Bruce followed him into the gym.

"You want me to take them from you?" Bruce threatened. Tugging the fake beard to his neck, he showed the other man he was serious.

"Oh, yeah," Estrada said, accepting the challenge.

The boys' basketball team had started to wander in for practice. Dan wheeled his chair to the middle of the court and started tossing out basketballs to the boys.

Dan threw one to Bruce. "Play for it. And I'm not going to make it easy for you."

"You're in a wheelchair."

Dan shrugged. "You only have one leg. I figure that makes us even."

The Marine Corps reserves and volunteers, here to hand out toys, and basketball players started to gather to see what the heck was going on in the gym.

Bruce looked for Henry, who'd been shadowing him all week. "Lend me your wheels."

"I got me a date," he said. "You're going to make me late."

"I'll give you a ride."

Henry stood and a couple of the boys helped him over to the bench.

Bruce sat in the wheelchair and propped up his left leg, just like Dan, so that he wouldn't have an advantage over the other man.

The game was as physical as any game he'd played from a chair. Bruce had experience with wheelchair basketball on his side. But Dan had been coaching from his seat for weeks now.

The game was first to 21, with Dan in the lead 19-18. The other man wasn't going to let him win. He had to work for it. Bruce had the reserves, Henry and his brother cheering him on. While Dan had his team behind him cheering just as loudly.

Bruce scored a three-pointer to put it away, then wheeled alongside Dan. "Tickets," he demanded.

"She has them. She's probably down at the the-

ater now. You'd better hurry—you only have an
hour to get downtown."

Bruce cursed under his breath. What a waste of
time. He returned Henry's chair and jogged toward
the door.

"Where do you think you're going?" Henry
rolled after him. "What about my date?"

"Henry, I'm in a hurry."

"You're gonna want to slow down." The old man
handed Bruce the pawn ticket.

Bruce glanced at Keith. Okay, maybe he'd give it
to his brother someday, but not right this minute.

"There's a watch and a ring waiting for you."

Bruce didn't just slow down—he stopped. "I
could kiss you."

MITZI PACED OUTSIDE the historic Ellie Caulkins
Opera House for the Colorado Ballet's *The Nutcracker.* No sign of Henry anywhere. She was now
worried that the stubborn old man's insistence that
he could get here on his own meant he'd gotten lost.
Sure, he knew his way around downtown. But had
Henry ever even been to a theater?

Only Lincoln Center in New York City was
bigger than Denver's twelve-acre group of theaters
known as the Denver Performing Arts Complex.
The buildings varied from exposed-beam contem-
porary at one end to the beautiful brownstone, in

front of which she now stood, completed in time for the 1908 Democratic National Convention.

Getting colder by the minute, she pulled her coat tighter. She'd worn a black cocktail dress and heels for the occasion.

She didn't want to miss this performance and debated entering the theater without him. But since she held both tickets, she decided to wait. The thought of starting a new holiday tradition— seeing *The Nutcracker* alone—sounded depressing. If Henry blew her off tonight he was going to get an earful.

She'd had enough of men blowing her off.

Calhoun hadn't returned a single call. She'd even resorted to sending him a test message.

Where are you?

Not at home. Not at the office.

She'd looked for that red Ford Escalade everywhere she could think to look. Surely with those eagle, globe and anchor hubcaps his SUV would stand out.

There was the rumor going around that he'd returned to recruiting duty. She'd have to hear it from him before she'd believe it. And she very much wanted to *believe* that he'd returned not just because he had orders, but because he wanted to. And dare she hope, for her?

If that was the case, where was he?

Sure, she owed him an apology. Enlisting his brother behind his back. When she should have been upfront about it. But the truth was she hadn't had much choice in the matter. Keith was always going to enlist.

Mitzi checked her watch and sighed. She couldn't give him much longer. As snowflakes started to fall, the holiday lights appeared brighter somehow.

"Look, Dad!" The little girl in front of her pointed. "Santa Claus!"

Mitzi whirled around to check out this amazing sight and came face-to-face with Calhoun. In a Santa suit.

Under his arm he carried a double-wide shoe box with a big red bow. Henry tagged along in his wheelchair. He wore an elfish-looking hat she could only hope he hadn't found in a Dumpster.

"You've been a very naughty girl while I've been gone," Santa said.

She gasped, prepared to argue. But the twinkle in his eye gave her pause.

"This is for you." He presented her with the oversize shoe box.

Mitzi opened it to find twenty years of memories, some happy, some sad, in a pair of red cowgirl boots. Her size.

"They're perfect." She reminded herself to breathe.

"I was *always* going to come back for you, Mitz."

She tilted her head to look at him. And saw the truth in his eyes.

"After Freddie was killed..." He shook his head. "I was a mess. Barely able to hold myself up. I'm a Marine. I'm supposed to be strong enough to carry you when you need me to. It tore me up inside knowing I wasn't. That's why I let you leave to come home—okay, made you leave," he admitted. "So you'd get that love and support you needed from family and friends."

He dropped his forehead to hers. "Forgive me?"

"I wanted to be there *for you*." She brushed his snow-white beard. "Sometime, Marine, you've got to let me rescue you. It's not just my job. It's an adventure. And my calling."

"Yeah, your job." He took a deep breath. "That's something we're going to have to talk about, Chief. I can't believe you reenlisted to go back to SAR."

"I wanted to be closer to you." She'd rather have that piece of him than nothing at all.

"Well, I didn't reenlist to spend the next four years apart. So we're going to have to make some calls come Monday."

He took a step back from her and tossed his floppy Santa hat to Henry. Then his beard.

"What am I, your valet now?" Henry grumbled.

Underneath the red-and-white fur-lined Santa suit, Calhoun wore his Marine Corps dress blues.

"Nice uniform, Master Sergeant," she said, calling attention to his new rank insignia and obvious promotion.

"You do know, Chief, this means you have to call me Master."

"Maybe, *Sergeant*."

Henry handed him his white hat and Calhoun put it on—his eyes never leaving hers. And hers never leaving his. Henry handed him a little black box.

"Is that—"

She stopped herself as Calhoun struggled to get down on his one good knee in front of the Ellie Caulkins Opera House. She fought back tears.

"Don't cry, sweetheart. It's just a leg. If that's all it cost to return to you I'd gladly give my other one."

She would have helped him to the ground, but the look he gave her stopped her. Some things never changed. "You can help me up," he said. "But only after you've said yes. Otherwise, I'm staying put."

"First I have to listen to all the mush," Henry

complained. "Now you're proposing to my date?" Apparently the crowd that gathered didn't feel the same way. They applauded.

"She's not your date tonight, old man. She's mine."

"I asked you was you Mitzi's Marine the first day we met."

"Hell, yes, I'm Mitzi's Marine," he said, opening the ring box. "If she'll have me?"

"That's my ring," Mitzi said.

"Can you see yourself married to a Marine? I'm not promising you it will be easy. With all the hardships and heartaches that come with it. But I am pledging love, honor and commitment for the rest of my life." Calhoun took a deep breath. "Mitzi, will you marry me?"

Was there ever any doubt?

"*Semper fi,* Marine!"

EPILOGUE

May Day
Four years later...

BRUCE AND HIS PARTNER were on bike patrol along Englewood's South Platte River trails near City Center and Cushing Park. With yesterday's snow just a memory, bikers and bladers were out in full force.

They'd dismounted to stop a dog walker.

"Officer Calhoun!" A group of middle school boys came rushing up. "Can we get your trading card?"

Bruce removed his sunglasses, hanging them on the V of his polo shirt, and kicked the stand in place for his all-terrain patrol bike. The Englewood Police Department had a trading card program for elementary through middle grades, to get kids used to the idea of approaching police officers.

The cards for him and his partner, Gregg Kello, were two of the more popular ones.

But Officer Kello was busy ticketing an irate dog owner for noncompliance when she refused to pick up poop.

"Shouldn't you boys be in school?" Bruce asked, reaching into his back pocket for the requested cards. He pulled out three and handed one to each of them.

Today's uniform consisted of a bike helmet, light blue polo shirt with a printed badge and navy blue shorts. It was the shorts that got him recognized every time.

"What happened to your leg?" one of the boys asked.

"Iraq."

"A wreck?"

Remembering a similar conversation, Bruce chuckled. "It's a country in the Middle East. Don't they teach you that in school?"

All three nodded without a clue.

Across the river a woman screamed. "My camera!"

A skater whizzed past their position with the woman's camera, but on the opposite bank. Kello forgot about ticketing the dog walker and mounted his bike. They'd have to haul ass just to get to the next crossover.

"Stay with my bike," he said to the boys.

A quick assessment and Bruce ran toward the new crossover construction. Jumping the orange net barrier, he headed straight for the narrow beam that would put him right behind the kid.

"Damn it, Calhoun, what am I supposed to tell your wife when they're dragging downriver for your body?"

"Tell her it was just another day on the O-course!" he said without slowing down over the water. He leaped onto the opposite bank and kicked it into gear.

Dodging a collision with a jogger, Bruce could see the skater up ahead. The kid had plenty of pedestrian obstacles to slow him down and Bruce used the crowd parting in the skateboard's wake to his advantage.

Breathing hard, he continued his chase.

The kid's near collision with a woman and a double-wide baby jogger gave Bruce pause. A camera wasn't worth an injured civilian. But in going around that stroller the skater's wheels met dirt. The kid lost momentum and stumbled off his board, quickly kicking it back to the pavement.

That misstep gave Bruce the opening he needed.

In a running dive worthy of any college football player, he brought the kid down. Pinning him with his good knee, he held him in an arm bar while he reached for his handcuffs. "You have the right to remain silent…"

After he cuffed the skater and read him his

rights, he strapped the camera over his shoulder and hauled the kid to his feet. Bruce stomped on the end of the board to kick it up so he didn't have to bend.

"Bet you didn't think I knew that trick."

"Who knew you could even run?" the skater said. "Who are you, RoboCop?"

"That's right," Kello said, braking to a stop on his patrol bike. "He's our very own RoboCop. And one hell of a lousy bowler."

"Where've you been?" Bruce asked as they headed toward the parking lot and their black-and-white. About the time they got the skater settled into the backseat, the three middle school boys showed up, walking Bruce's patrol bike for him. Followed by the tourist who'd had her camera snatched.

While Kello took the victim's statement, Bruce thanked the kids for their help. He took their names and the name of their school so he could acknowledge them in front of all their friends with junior citations.

Then they loaded their bikes onto the bike rack and headed over to City Center to book the twenty-two-year-old.

"THEN HE CALLED CALHOUN RoboCop," Kello said, filling their bowling team in on the details

as they waited for the fire department's team, the
Ball Burners, to show up.

Bruce looked up from tying his bowling shoes.
"Enough, already."

They'd named their team Strike Force. All military, all cops. All the time. Bruce had settled into
civilian life as a reservist. And that suited him just
fine.

Walking in with a cane and a slight limp, Henry
sat at the table behind their lane. As he did every
Wednesday night to watch them bowl.

Stepping up to Henry's level, Bruce signaled the
staff to bring a beer for his favorite old goat. There
were advantages to owning the place.

"Have you seen the Chief tonight?" he asked
Henry.

"What am I, her keeper? Thought that was your
job?"

"Better not let her hear you say that."

"Hear you say what?" Mitzi asked, slipping her
arm through Bruce's. "Sorry I'm late," she said to
him. "A Labrador fell into a frozen pond at shift
change." She looked to Henry expectantly.

"Just making sure Calhoun's taking care of you,"
Henry grumbled.

Mitzi indulged them both with a smile. "Hmm,"
she said, remembering something. "You haven't
seen the picture of our babies yet." She dug the

ultrasound out of her back pocket and handed it to Henry.

"You didn't go in the water after it?" Bruce frowned at her, putting a protective hand to the slight swell of her belly. "The dog?"

"It wasn't that cold, Calhoun," she teased. "No." She rubbed his flat belly in return. "You know I'm on restricted duty until after the twins are born."

Two babies.

As if that wasn't enough to worry him.

His wife had to be an EMT with Fire Rescue.

"Hmm," she said, remembering something. "We got an email from Keith."

"Did he pass his MCAT?"

"We're going to have a doctor in the family."

Turned out Keith was a damn fine Marine. Well, Navy corpsman serving with the Marine Corps. Mitzi had worked her magic and opened up a world of opportunity for him with the Navy. After completing all his college requirements for premed while on active duty he was headed to medical school on Uncle Sam's dime.

Granted, he was going to be obligated to the United States Navy for a very long time. Still, med school.

"Calhoun, you're up next," Kate Sloan called from the lanes. He'd been oblivious to the sound of falling pins. Their two teams played in a mixed league, and every now and then, like tonight, they were up against each other.

"Just like old times." He leaned down to kiss his wife before he beat the pants off her at bowling.

"Something's wrong with this picture." Henry handed the ultrasound to Bruce. Bruce stared at it. He'd been there when they took it, and for all Mitzi's appointments. The doctor said they had two healthy babies. What was the old man seeing that he wasn't?

"I know it's hard to make out because they're twins—" Mitzi started.

"Nothing hard about it," the old man grumbled. "I see two of everything. Calhoun, if I were you I'd insist on a paternity test."

"Henry—"

He cut her off. "They couldn't possibly be Calhoun's. They're both coming out with two legs."

Bruce chuckled. "It's an amputee joke, sweetheart."

"I get it!" she said. "You can forget about us asking you to be a godparent, old man."

"Good, because I know what that means, and I didn't want to get stuck with diaper duty anyway."

"Fine." Mitzi dragged Bruce toward their lane and waiting teammates.

"Fine, yourself," Henry said.

"They're going to love him." She smiled up at Bruce.

"You know it." He dropped a kiss on her forehead. "Not as much as I love you."

"I love you, too."

"Oh, come on, you two," Kello said. "It's not like you work different shifts and haven't seen each other in four days."

Which was exactly what it was like. Better together than apart.

* * * * *

Harlequin® Super Romance®

COMING NEXT MONTH

Available June 14, 2011

#1710 FINDING HER DAD
Suddenly a Parent
Janice Kay Johnson

#1711 MARRIED BY JUNE
Make Me a Match
Ellen Hartman

#1712 HER BEST FRIEND'S WEDDING
More than Friends
Abby Gaines

#1713 HONOR BOUND
Count on a Cop
Julianna Morris

#1714 TWICE THE CHANCE
Twins
Darlene Gardner

#1715 A RISK WORTH TAKING
Zana Bell

You can find more information on upcoming Harlequin® titles, free excerpts and more at
www.HarlequinInsideRomance.com.

REQUEST YOUR FREE BOOKS!
2 FREE NOVELS PLUS 2 FREE GIFTS!

Harlequin®

Super Romance®

Exciting, emotional, unexpected!

YES! Please send me 2 FREE Harlequin® Superromance® novels and my 2 FREE gifts (gifts are worth about $10). After receiving them, if I don't wish to receive any more books, I can return the shipping statement marked "cancel." If I don't cancel, I will receive 6 brand-new novels every month and be billed just $4.69 per book in the U.S. or $5.24 per book in Canada. That's a saving of at least 15% off the cover price! It's quite a bargain! Shipping and handling is just 50¢ per book in the U.S. and 75¢ per book in Canada.* I understand that accepting the 2 free books and gifts places me under no obligation to buy anything. I can always return a shipment and cancel at any time. Even if I never buy another book, the two free books and gifts are mine to keep forever.

135/336 HDN FC6T

Name	(PLEASE PRINT)	
Address		Apt. #
City	State/Prov.	Zip/Postal Code

Signature (if under 18, a parent or guardian must sign)

Mail to the Reader Service:
IN U.S.A.: P.O. Box 1867, Buffalo, NY 14240-1867
IN CANADA: P.O. Box 609, Fort Erie, Ontario L2A 5X3

Not valid for current subscribers to Harlequin Superromance books.
**Are you a current subscriber to Harlequin Superromance books
and want to receive the larger-print edition?
Call 1-800-873-8635 or visit www.ReaderService.com.**

* Terms and prices subject to change without notice. Prices do not include applicable taxes. Sales tax applicable in N.Y. Canadian residents will be charged applicable taxes. Offer not valid in Quebec. This offer is limited to one order per household. All orders subject to credit approval. Credit or debit balances in a customer's account(s) may be offset by any other outstanding balance owed by or to the customer. Please allow 4 to 6 weeks for delivery. Offer available while quantities last.

Your Privacy—The Reader Service is committed to protecting your privacy. Our Privacy Policy is available online at www.ReaderService.com or upon request from the Reader Service.

We make a portion of our mailing list available to reputable third parties that offer products we believe may interest you. If you prefer that we not exchange your name with third parties, or if you wish to clarify or modify your communication preferences, please visit us at www.ReaderService.com/consumerschoice or write to us at Reader Service Preference Service, P.O. Box 9062, Buffalo, NY 14269. Include your complete name and address.

HSR11

Harlequin® Blaze™ brings you
New York Times *and* USA TODAY *bestselling author*
Vicki Lewis Thompson with three new steamy titles
from the bestselling miniseries SONS OF CHANCE

Chance isn't just the last name of these rugged
Wyoming cowboys—it's their motto, too!

Read on for a sneak peek at the first title,
SHOULD'VE BEEN A COWBOY

Available June 2011 only from Harlequin® Blaze™.

"THANKS FOR NOT TURNING ON THE LIGHTS," Tyler said. "I'm a mess."

"Not in my book." Even in low light, Alex had a good view of her yellow shirt plastered to her body. It was all he could do not to reach for her, mud and all. But the next move needed to be hers, not his.

She slicked her wet hair back and squeezed some water out of the ends as she glanced upward. "I like the sound of the rain on a tin roof."

"Me, too."

She met his gaze briefly and looked away. "Where's the sink?"

"At the far end, beyond the last stall."

Tyler's running shoes squished as she walked down the aisle between the rows of stalls. She glanced sideways at Alex. "So how much of a cowboy are you these days? Do you ride the range and stuff?"

"I ride." He liked being able to say that. "Why?"

"Just wondered. Last summer, you were still a city boy. You even told me you weren't the cowboy type, but you're...different now."

He wasn't sure if that was a good thing or a bad thing. Maybe she preferred city boys to cowboys. "How am I different?"

"Well, you dress differently, and your hair's a little longer. Your face seems a little more chiseled, but maybe that's because of your hair. Also, there's something else, something harder to define, an attitude…"

"Are you saying I have an attitude?"

"Not in a bad way. It's more like a quiet confidence."

He was flattered, but still he had to laugh. "I just admitted a while ago that I have all kinds of doubts about this event tomorrow. That doesn't seem like quiet confidence to me."

"This isn't about your job, it's about…your…" She took a deep breath. "It's about your sex appeal, okay? I have no business talking about it, because it will only make me want to do things I shouldn't do." She started toward the end of the barn. "Now, where's that sink? We need to get cleaned up and go back to the house. Dinner is probably ready, and I—"

He spun her around and pulled her into his arms, mud and all. "Let's do those things." Then he kissed her, knowing that she would kiss him back, knowing that this time he would take that kiss where he wanted it to go. And she would let him.

Follow Tyler and Alex's wild adventures in
SHOULD'VE BEEN A COWBOY
Available June 2011 only from Harlequin® Blaze™
wherever books are sold.

Finding Her Dad

Janice Kay Johnson

Jonathan Brenner was busy running for office as county sheriff. The last thing on his mind was parenthood...that is, until a resourceful, awkward teenage girl shows up claiming to be his daughter!

Available June
wherever books are sold.

www.eHarlequin.com

HSR71710

SPECIAL EDITION

Life, Love and Family

LOVE CAN BE FOUND IN THE MOST UNLIKELY PLACES, ESPECIALLY WHEN YOU'RE NOT LOOKING FOR IT...

Failed marriages, broken families and disappointment. Cecilia and Brandon have both been unlucky in love and life and are ripe for an intervention. Good thing Brandon's mother happens to stumble upon this matchmaking project. But will Brandon be able to open his eyes and get away from his busy career to see that all he needs is right there in front of him?

FIND OUT IN

WHAT THE SINGLE DAD WANTS...

BY *USA TODAY* BESTSELLING AUTHOR

MARIE FERRARELLA

AVAILABLE IN JUNE 2011
WHEREVER BOOKS ARE SOLD.

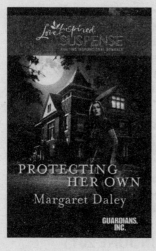